I0570652

Books by Helena Stone

Dublin Virtues

Patience
Equality
Renewal

Single Titles

Little Rainbows
Scenes from Adelaide Road

Renewal

ISBN # 978-1-78686-178-8

©Copyright Helena Stone 2017

Cover Art by Posh Gosh ©Copyright 2017

Interior text design by Claire Siemaszkiewicz

Pride Publishing

This is a work of fiction. All characters, places and events are from the author's imagination and should not be confused with fact. Any resemblance to persons, living or dead, events or places is purely coincidental.

All rights reserved. No part of this publication may be reproduced in any material form, whether by printing, photocopying, scanning or otherwise without the written permission of the publisher, Pride Publishing.

Applications should be addressed in the first instance, in writing, to Pride Publishing. Unauthorised or restricted acts in relation to this publication may result in civil proceedings and/or criminal prosecution.

The author and illustrator have asserted their respective rights under the Copyright Designs and Patents Acts 1988 (as amended) to be identified as the author of this book and illustrator of the artwork.

Published in 2017 by Pride Publishing, Think Tank, Ruston Way, Lincoln, LN6 7FL, United Kingdom.

No part of this book may be reproduced, scanned, or distributed in any printed or electronic form without permission. Please do not participate in or encourage piracy of copyrighted materials in violation of the authors' rights. Purchase only authorised copies.

Pride Publishing is a subsidiary of Totally Entwined Group Limited.

If you purchased this book without a cover you should be aware that this book is stolen property. It was reported as "unsold and destroyed" to the publisher and neither the author nor the publisher has received any payment for this "stripped book".

Dublin Virtues

RENEWAL

HELENA STONE

Dedication

This book is for Chris. For reasons.

Chapter One

Shane accepted his change from the barman, picked up his pint and turned around. The pub was all but deserted and he had his choice of empty tables. Hardly surprising, given that it was eight o'clock on a Wednesday evening, but that didn't lessen the small stab of disappointment he felt. The first opportunity he'd had to go out in three weeks, probably the last in the foreseeable future, and not a familiar face in sight.

Not that he necessarily wanted to run into anybody who knew him well. He'd rather not answer questions about why he was never around these days. On the other hand, he desperately needed a distraction, something to take his mind off the situation he found himself in. A vaguely familiar face, somebody he could join and pass an hour or two with without running the risk of the conversation turning heavy or personal would have been perfect – and clearly wasn't happening tonight. A hook-up was even less likely and he could do with one. It had been months since he'd gotten off through means other than his own hand.

He pushed the thought to the back of his mind as he glanced around again, trying to figure out where to take his drink. The idea of sitting at one of the round tables on his own filled him with a heaviness he didn't want to explore. Shane pulled a barstool toward himself with his foot and sat. Staring into the mirror behind the bar, he took a long drink from his glass as he remembered the scene he'd left behind at home.

'Where you're going, Uncle Shane?' Five-year-old Danny had sounded close to tears even before Shane answered.

'Out for a drink, boy.' Shane had stroked the still-wet blond hair.

'Are you coming back?' The big tears welling in Danny's eyes had almost made him reconsider his idea. He couldn't blame the child for no longer trusting the adults in his life to come back after they left. He'd knelt and made sure to make eye contact before answering.

'Of course I'll come back. We're in this together, right?' He'd forced a smile in the hope it would quell the lad's growing panic. 'When you wake up tomorrow morning I'll be making you breakfast. Just as I did today. I promise. Besides, don't you like it when your granny minds you? Doesn't she let you stay up late?'

The combination of a triumphant smile and tears on the five year old's face had almost broken Shane's resolve. Christ, but I love the nipper.

'On you go, son.' His mother's voice had put an end to the conversation with Danny. 'Don't you worry about anything at all. Go and enjoy yourself for a while.'

'Sure, Ma, thanks. Don't keep him up too late.' He'd given Danny a hug and a kiss before getting up and walking out of the door, grateful for his mother's support. The situation was even harder on her than it was for Shane and not for the first time he wondered how long she'd be able to keep up the pace.

Irritated with himself, Shane picked up his pint again and drank some more. Spending his evening worrying about the situation at home defeated the purpose of the exercise. He was supposed to get a short reprieve from it all. Wallowing in the pain and stress wouldn't get him anywhere. In fact, if he couldn't force his thoughts away from pursuing the subject, he might as well go back home. At least there he'd have something to do, which meant his mind was less likely to go over the whole sorry situation in a never-ending loop.

He finished his pint and immediately waved the bartender over to order another one. Too bad he couldn't allow himself to get drunk. But he'd tried going through the early morning routine with Danny while hungover once, and it wasn't something he wanted to repeat.

"That's quite a frown you've got on your face, mate."

Shane glanced up from the spot on the counter he'd apparently switched his attention to at some point and turned to his left, only to discover he needed to tilt his head back in order to look the man who'd addressed him in the face. *Fuck, the geezer is big.* At a loss about what to say in response to what was clearly a statement of fact, Shane took his time to study the man-mountain smiling down at him. He had to be at least two meters tall, with broad shoulders and a wide chest. Shane didn't think there was a lot of fat on that body though — just bones and muscle.

"You're on your own too?" the man asked. "Mind if I join you? Drinking on my own always makes me feel kinda desperate."

"Sure." Shane nodded in the direction of the empty barstool next to him. "Help yourself." He noticed the accent and tried to place it. "Australian, are you?"

"Yeah," The man's friendly features stretched into a grin. "Thanks for getting it right, mate. I'm so tired of people asking me if I'm American, I can't begin to tell you. I'm Chris."

"Shane," he responded. "I lived in the States up to five months ago. I knew you weren't American as soon as you opened your mouth."

Shit. Why had he said that? He didn't talk about his time in Florida with anyone — not about going there, not about coming back and not about the reasons why he'd needed to return. There was too much shame and pain in those stories to share them with others.

Shane picked up his pint while sending up a silent prayer Chris wouldn't ask him about his time on the other side of the Atlantic and thanking his lucky stars when the bartender picked that moment to come and take Chris' order.

He was nothing like the type of man Shane was normally attracted to. Sure, he liked his men tall and handsome — both of which Chris was — but Chris was too close to a bear.

Shane's preference ran to slimmer builds and he wasn't a huge fan of facial hair. On the other hand, he couldn't deny that the short dark brown hair dotted with tiny hints of gray was attractive, as was the goatee which covered Chris' chin but did nothing to obscure his full lips. Glasses usually didn't do anything for Shane either but they suited Chris and made his dark gray eyes sparkle.

When Chris raised one eyebrow, Shane averted his gaze and reached for his pint, disgusted to have been caught staring. What was wrong with him? Sure, it had been a long time—too long—since he'd flirted with a man, never mind picked one up. That wasn't an excuse for looking and acting desperate though.

"Have you been in Ireland long, then?" Shane asked in the hope a conversation would distract both of them from his less than subtle perusal of Chris.

"Almost ten years," Chris answered. "Came here for a few months to visit family and just never left again."

"What made you stay?" Much to his own surprise, Shane was really curious to hear the answer to that question. "I can't imagine it was the weather."

Chris threw back his head and laughed, the sound deep and clearly genuine.

"The Irish climate is nothing to write home about, that's for sure," Chris agreed. "Mind you, the heat in Australia didn't agree with me either. If I had to choose I'd take the mild but wet weather over the oppressive heat." He winked. "I guess that's exactly what I did when I decided to stay."

The both picked up their glasses and drank in silence for a few moments.

"I like your ink," Chris said while studying Shane's arm.

Shane followed his gaze and stared at the Celtic design covering most of his right arm. "Thank you." He couldn't keep the pride out of his voice. "I designed the pattern myself."

"You did?" Surprise flashed across Chris' face before being replaced by a look of delight. "You're a tattoo artist too?"

"I am," Shane confirmed. "And since you said *too*, I guess the same is true for you?"

Chris nodded. "Yes, have been for almost fifteen years now. It's the only real job I've ever had."

Shane lowered his gaze and studied Chris' forearms, only to find no sign of a tattoo anywhere. "But you've no tattoos yourself?" Shane couldn't imagine a tattooist without art on his own body but he guessed there was a probably a first time for everything.

Chris studied his own arms for a moment before answering. "None where people can see them. My mother had issues with tattoos, among other things."

"Oh?" Shane left it hanging there in the hope Chris would say more.

"You'll need to get to know me a lot better before you find out where exactly I do have art." Chris smirked before tracing a finger along the lines of the Celtic cross on Shane's biceps.

He couldn't suppress a shudder. It had been so long— too long—since anybody had touched him in a meaningful way. "Want another pint?" Shane hated the tremble in his voice when he asked the question.

"Not right now." Chris lifted his gaze while he continued to stroke Shane's arm with his finger. He glanced over Shane's shoulder in the direction of the hallway leading to the toilets and beer garden, before quirking an eyebrow at Shane.

Shane swallowed hard before nodding and getting off his barstool. He'd no idea why he was nervous. This used to be standard fare in the past. Rushed encounters in dark corners and quick fucks in the rooms of men he'd forget as soon as he left had been his normal until recently. Why the fuck did it suddenly feel like a big deal?

He forced himself to walk slowly, all too aware of the presence behind him. When he slowed down as they neared the toilets a soft push against his lower back made him continue through the backdoor and into the balmy August evening air. When he came to a standstill, Chris leaned into him and whispered in his ear. "Just around the corner there."

Glancing to the right, he saw the small path and followed it until they'd rounded the corner and found themselves in a side garden. He opened his mouth to ask where to go next and forgot the question when Chris grabbed his shoulder, pulled him around and shoved him up against the wall. Shane's heart skipped a beat as he realized he was all alone with a man big enough to squash him if he felt like it. He forced himself to meet Chris' gaze and got caught in the hungry, heated stare from his eyes.

"I..."

Chris lowered his head and captured Shane's lips with his. Since he'd no idea what he would have said if he'd been allowed to finish his sentence, Shane didn't even pretend to object and allowed himself to respond with equal urgency. It *had* been too long. It felt too good. He'd hardly ever kissed the men he'd picked up in the past—the short-lived encounters he preferred had never warranted that level of intimacy. Right now, he couldn't for the life of him remember why that had ever made sense.

He closed his eyes and lost himself in the play of their lips, relishing the way Chris' goatee scratched and tickled his clean-shaven chin. The small sounds escaping his mouth and betraying his need should have embarrassed him but only spurred him on. Given that Chris' hand was suddenly on his crotch, unzipping his fly, he imagined the feeling was mutual.

Shane's mind switched off. He'd always been the one to take charge and control of proceedings in the past. Tonight he was more than happy to relinquish control to the big Australian—delighted to just take whatever happened to be on offer. Warm air brushed across the skin of his hard and now released cock and he shuddered. The sound of a second zip opening took him by surprise, but he resisted the temptation to open his eyes. When a large hand surrounded his dick and pressed it against an equally rigid cock, he opened his mouth wider and released a groan which felt as though it came from his toes, grateful that Chris' mouth, still crushing his, captured most of the sound.

Shane was dimly aware that Chris' hand was big enough to fully encircle both their cocks. The first few strokes, the way their dicks rubbed off each other and the slight squeezes and twists Chris applied drove Shane mad. He could already feel his balls drawing up and knew he wouldn't last long. The thought shot through his head that he should ask Chris to slow down but he couldn't make himself pull back from their never-ending kiss. His orgasm roared through his body, satisfying him in ways a solitary hand job had never been able to do. Chris didn't stop his movements and stroked Shane through his orgasm and beyond until Shane's knees didn't feel strong enough to hold him up anymore.

"Fuck yeah." Chris mumbled the heartfelt words against Shane's lips as he too erupted.

The kiss ended as soon as Chris' orgasm had passed. For a moment he pulled Shane close, holding both of them up as they regained their breath and Shane managed to find a semblance of his equilibrium again. When Chris released him, pushing his softening dick back into his pants and zipping up, Shane did the same. He'd no idea why he felt both fully satisfied and deeply disappointed and ignored the question. This encounter had been more and much better than anything he could have hoped for. He'd be a fool to question it.

When Chris turned and walked back in the direction of the entrance to the pub, Shane followed.

"Thirsty work," Chris said without turning around.

Shane tried to swallow and found his throat was uncomfortably dry. "Yes, thirsty work indeed. I guess that means you're ready for that pint now?"

Chapter Two

Chris bit down hard on the fifth yawn in as many minutes while contemplating walking into Costa Coffee for a large flat white. A quick glance at his watch told him he'd no time for that luxury right now. He couldn't afford to be late today of all days. He'd just have to hope they'd have copious amounts of caffeine ready and waiting when he arrived.

Maybe he shouldn't have gone out last night. Maybe it was time to accept that he wasn't as young as he used to be. Ten years ago a late night, or even a sleepless one, wouldn't have bothered him. Today he felt shattered. Not that he'd stayed out too late. He'd had one further drink with Shane while they'd tried to keep a slightly uncomfortable and definitely forced conversation going, before Shane had announced he needed to go home.

Chris yawned again as he remembered the disappointment he'd felt when Shane had refused to exchange phone numbers. The unexpected emotion had been the last of several surprising developments the previous evening. He still wasn't sure what had possessed him to approach the man he'd seen sitting at the bar, never mind why he'd thought it would be a good idea to take him outside for the quick hand job. His cock stirred in his pants. *Quick but very memorable.*

He tried to remember the last time he'd been as impulsive and realized it had been almost two years since he'd indulged in a quickie in public. Sure, he'd enjoyed hookups in the meantime, but more often than not with partners he'd known at least vaguely and they'd always taken it to a bedroom.

There'd been something about Shane. The way he'd frowned at his pint had pulled Chris in his direction as if it was his duty to make the man feel better.

Suddenly irritated with himself and his fanciful ideas, Chris turned the corner. Just a few more minutes and he'd reach his destination. It would have helped if he'd had a decent night's sleep and he wasn't quite sure why he hadn't. He never had any issues falling or staying asleep so why it would have been such a struggle last night was a mystery. But he'd tossed and turned as his mind switched from his encounter with Shane to wondering about what to expect in the morning. At least that last question would be answered shortly, even if he'd never figure out what it was about Shane that had gotten to him.

'VikInk.' He read the name on the sign hanging over a door just a few meters away and stopped walking for a moment as he went over the conversation he'd had with Troy, his employer, a few days ago.

'I've got a favor to ask, Chris. Feel free to say no if you don't want to do it.'

'Sure, what's the favor?' Chris asked.

'Barry, the man I used to work for before I opened this place, asked me for help. He's got two of his tattooists out at the same time unexpectedly and needs an extra set of hands. I'd do it myself, but…'

Chris understood. 'But this is your parlor and it makes sense for you to be here. What do you need me to do?'

'There's that. And then there's…never mind. Here's the story. Barry would like to borrow you one day a week for a month. He says he can shuffle his remaining staff around the rest of the time but since he's open seven days a week, there's only so much reorganizing he can do.'

'And you're sure you can do without me here one day a week?' Chris asked. 'Because I don't really want to add a sixth working day to my week.'

'No!' Troy looked horrified. 'Nobody is expecting you to work *more hours than you already do. It will take some careful planning but I can't see it being a problem if it's only one day per week.'*

'And you clearly want to help your old employer out,' Chris said.

'Yes. I mean, I didn't exactly leave on agreeable terms but we've since made our peace and it doesn't hurt to have a good working relationship with at least one of the other parlors. It's not impossible we'll find ourselves in a similar position at some point in the future.'

When he'd agreed to the proposition Chris had been excited at the idea of working somewhere else occasionally. Different parlors often had different styles and it would be good to spread his wings and maybe find new inspiration.

What had kept him awake last night hadn't been happy anticipation about diving into a new venture so much as worry about all the ways in which it could go wrong. What if he didn't get on with this Barry or the other people working there? What if they didn't allow him to work the way he was used to? What if…? As he'd tried to do last night, Chris shut down the questions running through his head. It was too late for those now anyway. He'd arrived at his destination.

He entered the parlor and went straight to the counter, paying little attention to the layout of the place or the people already there.

"Can I help you?" The man asking the question looked to be in his mid-forties.

"Chris Anderson," he said. "I think you're expecting me."

A smile spread across the man's face. "Yes, I am. Thank you for helping us out. I'm Barry, by the way. Follow me and I'll show you around."

Much to Chris' surprise, Barry didn't lead him straight to the tattoo stations but headed for the other side of the parlor first.

"This here is the staff-room-cum-kitchen. Coffee" — Barry pointed at the machine on a counter — "is kept going all day. If you take the last cup you refill the machine and start a new pot."

Chris grinned. "Do you mind if I help myself to a mug? I could do with one."

"Sure, work away." Barry leaned against the wall while Chris grabbed the largest mug he could find and filled it with coffee, forgoing the milk he usually took in favor of a greater caffeine hit. He sipped the hot liquid, suppressing a satisfied sigh before turning around to face Barry again and following him back onto the shop floor.

"This is Ciara."

Chris nodded at the girl with jet-black spiky hair before following Barry to the next tattoo station. In what felt like record time, Barry introduced him to three other tattooists before stopping next to an empty station. "This will be yours when you're here. Did you bring your own machine or…?

"Of course." Chris shrugged off his backpack and lowered it to the floor while wondering why any self-respecting tattoo artist would work with a machine not his own. If he had no other choice he could, of course, but there was nothing quite like working with the machine he was used to, the one that fitted his hand just right.

"Ah, there you are. I wondered where you'd disappeared to."

Busy pulling his equipment from the bag, Chris only saw the approaching shoes of the person Barry had been addressing. When he looked up his breathing faltered for a moment as soon as he recognized the man those feet belonged to.

"This is Shane. Shane, meet Chris. He'll be manning the station next to yours once a week and, as I said, I'm expecting you to give him any assistance he needs. If you'll excuse me, I've got a few things that need taking care of." Barry turned and walked away without waiting for an answer, unaware of the blush on Shane's face and Chris' shock.

Finding himself lost for words, Chris just stared at Shane.

What were the chances of this being the same man he'd shared an orgasm with last night? But that was who stood in front of him. The same shaggy blond hair featuring bleached tips as the last evidence of an old coloring job. The same kissable lips, although right now they were thin and, like the rest of Shane's face, drawn into an angry scowl.

"You have got to be fucking kidding me! Am I to believe this is a coincidence?" Shane angrily hissed the words at Chris.

"Eh…yeah." Chris had no idea what could have caused the sudden anger Shane displayed.

"Give me a fucking break." If anything, Chris' denial seemed to only make Shane more furious. "You work for Troy, right? That's where Barry said he'd found a temp."

"I do," Chris answered. "What's that got to do with anything?"

"Oh please. Don't treat me as if I'm stupid. I'm well aware Troy's upset with me and God knows he's every right to be. I just didn't think he'd sink this low."

"I have no idea what you're talking about." Chris tried to keep a hold on the confusion-fed anger he could feel bubbling up inside him. "I'm kinda freaked out to run into you here after our encounter last night, if that's what you mean. But I don't see what Troy has got to do with any of that."

Shane studied him in silence for a few long moments and Chris waited for whatever might be coming next. An explanation would've been nice because he suddenly felt certain that he was at the distinct disadvantage of not having all necessary information.

"You really don't know."

Since it wasn't a question, Chris didn't respond.

Shane's cheeks heated again. "Ask Troy next time you see him. I'm sure he'll be happy to explain it all to you. I…I'm sorry I lost it there. You're right, this is awkward. And it's bound to get more so after you've spoken with Troy, but I guess we'll just have to get on with it for the few days you'll be working here."

Chris wanted to press the issue. He hated the idea that he'd walked into what was clearly an uncomfortable situation without having a clue what was going on, but one look at Shane's face warned him to bide his time. He could and would talk to Troy tomorrow. And if his boss had knowingly sent him into what could apparently easily turn into an impossible situation, he'd have it out with him.

"Fair enough," he said. "Are you going to tell me exactly what's on the agenda for me today? Barry didn't tell me anything."

"Sure." Shane took a deep breath, as if he needed to collect himself. "I'm afraid you'll only be dealing with small, quick jobs. It makes sense because you're only here one day a week and for a short time. There'd be no point in starting something requiring multiple sittings if you're not going to be here to do the later ones."

"Yeah, I figured as much," Chris said. "If I worked here full time that would get boring very quickly. Since that's not the case, it'll be fine."

"Chris!" Barry's voice rang through the parlor. "Come here for a moment, would you?"

"And so it begins." Chris smiled at Shane before turning away from him and walking to the reception counter where Barry waited for him with a youngish woman. Shane hadn't reacted to his smile at all and Chris was hard pressed to explain the disappointment he felt as a result.

Three hours later, Chris had to admit that even if he only worked here one day a week, it might well get boring before too long. So far, he'd placed a small heart on the woman, a shamrock on an American tourist and a semi-colon on a youngster who'd come in with his mother.

That last one had touched him. He knew only too well why people got that mark tattooed and it broke his heart to think that this young man—a child still, really—had already gone through enough hardship to have earned the right to wear it. To have contemplated or, God forbid,

17

attempted suicide at such a young age was a horrifying idea. Both the youngster and his mother had been quiet during the process, so he'd no idea what the story was and knew he had no right to ask, but not for the first time he wished there was more he could do than just set the tattoo.

"Okay, lads," Barry's voice broke through Chris' musings. "Since I have you two working together, more or less, you might as well take your lunch break at the same time. Please don't be late coming back. Both of you have an appointment at two." And he was gone again.

"Where do you usually go for your lunch?" Chris studied Shane as he asked the question and could predict his response before Shane opened his mouth.

"A coffee shop around the corner. But there's lots of good places to eat around here. There's absolutely no need for you to join me, just because we're having our break at the same time. In fact—"

"Don't be a dick." Chris' patience evaporated. They'd worked together very well all through the morning and he had no intention of allowing Shane to shut him out again. "I don't enjoy eating on my own if I don't have to. If we're going to be working together for four weeks, we might as well try to get along."

"As if that's going to last." Shane muttered the words as the two of them walked to the front of the shop and into the sunlit street.

"What's that supposed to mean?" Chris asked, exasperated.

"It's not as if you'll still want to have lunch with me after you've talked to Troy," Shane answered. "In fact, you'll probably be asking Barry to work with someone else when you come again next week."

"If you're so sure about that, why don't *you* tell me what's going on with you and Troy? Why drag it out?" The whole mystery was starting to get on Chris' nerves. For a moment, he contemplated calling Troy and demanding answers from him but he rejected the idea. Clearly Shane thought the issue — whatever it would turn out to be — was big enough to alienate Chris as soon as he heard the details. If it really was that bad he'd probably be better off waiting until he was face to face with Troy. He couldn't help feeling he was being played, possibly from two sides, and he didn't like the idea at all.

Chapter Three

Shane opened his mouth to tell Chris exactly what the issue between Troy and him was, only to close it again. As he led the way into the coffee shop he realized he really shouldn't be the first one to give the details to Chris. It was Troy's story. Shane had been a little shit at the time and he couldn't deny Troy had very good reasons to be upset with him. He also knew he wouldn't be able to tell the story without trying to come up with excuses for himself and his behavior, and that wouldn't be right either and would only make him look worse in the long run.

They walked to the long, glass-fronted counter and he studied Chris as he ordered himself a sandwich and a large coffee. The Australian clearly had a caffeine addiction, if the quantities in which he ingested the substance were anything to go by. He was also strangely attractive. Shane instantly closed the door on that thought. Even if it hadn't been for the whole Troy situation, now wasn't the time to fall for him, or anybody else for that matter. He had more than enough going on in his life without inviting more potentially complicated situations into it.

"My usual, please," Shane said to the man behind the counter when it was his turn to order. They paid for their lunches and made their way to a table in the far corner of the already busy place.

"Well," Chris said. "Are you going to put me out of my misery and tell me what's going on?"

Shane appreciated Chris' light tone. Despite the fact that Shane had been less than nice and only barely polite to Chris for most of the morning, the Australian was still friendly, almost teasing.

"I'm sorry, but I really think it's better if you hear the story from Troy." Shane stared at his hands on the table for a moment before continuing. "If—and it's a big if—you're still interested in what I have to say about it after you've spoken to Troy, I'll answer whatever questions you may have." He cringed internally as he listened to himself. If someone spoke to him in the sort of riddles he was throwing at Chris he'd probably lose his patience fast. He had to give Chris huge bonus points for not getting angry.

Of course, Chris wasn't the only one surprising him right now. Shane had no idea what'd come over him. Had he really just offered to talk about the whole sorry affair with Chris if he wanted that? And what was more, he'd actually meant it when he said the words... He still did. He barely recognized himself these days. He'd only returned from America five months ago. When he'd got off the plane he'd still been the same old Shane he'd always been—cocky and selfish, as his mother had been happy to point out to him on numerous occasions in the past. Now that he thought about it he realized even she hadn't pointed any of his faults out to him for a long time.

"...more curious."

"Sorry, what?" Shane stared at Chris, fully aware he'd zoned out while lost in his thoughts. *If only I didn't have so damn much on my mind...* He stopped himself before he forgot where he was for a second time.

"I said that the way you're avoiding the question is only making me more curious," Chris said.

"Trust me," Shane said, fully aware of the irony since he knew without a doubt that trusting him would be the last thing Chris would do once Troy had finished telling him all about Shane. "You'll understand my reasons once you've talked to him." He breathed a sigh of relief as their sandwiches and drinks were served at their table. He really didn't want to think or talk about Troy anymore. This would more than likely be the only time he had lunch with

Chris and he actually liked him, so he might as well enjoy his company while he could.

They ate in silence for a few minutes while Shane grew increasingly less comfortable. Chris' gaze never seemed to leave his face. When he'd taken his last bite, he couldn't take it anymore.

"What?" He picked up his serviette. "Do I have mayo on my cheek or something?"

Chris' generous mouth stretched into a smile and small lines appeared around his eyes. For the first time since he'd met him, Shane wondered how old Chris was. He had a few more years on him than Shane's twenty-seven, that much he knew for sure.

"No, your face is fine." The humor in his voice was mirrored in his expression. "I'm just trying to figure you out."

Shane shuddered as a feeling of discomfort crawled through his veins. "Why? I'm not that interesting."

"Oh, I think you're rather fascinating." Chris sat back in his chair and relaxed while continuing to observe Shane.

Is he flirting with me? Lost for words, Shane stared back. Protesting again would just make him sound as if he was fishing for compliments, but he honestly didn't understand what Chris could possibly be fascinated by. A few months ago it might have been a different story. Back then he'd still bleached or colored his hair and he'd never left his house without at least mascara on his lashes. Right now he couldn't even remember where he kept his makeup and his hair was too long, unruly and shoddy-looking. Which reminded him he had to find a free hour somewhere so he could get it cut. At least he wouldn't resemble an abandoned dog anymore once he'd gotten rid of the last remnants of bleached blond.

He really needed to come up with some sort of response since he felt more uncomfortable with every second passing in silence while Chris scrutinized him. When a ringtone sounded and Chris reached for his phone, Shane sent a silent thank you to whatever God had just thrown him a lifeline.

"Troy, what's this? Are you checking up on me?"

If Shane had thought he was uncomfortable before, his levels of discomfort reached new and never-before-experienced heights now.

"Now, that's fine. I'm on my lunch break right now, so I can take a call."

Shane wondered if he should walk away from the table while Chris was on the phone. Under any other circumstances the thought wouldn't have crossed his mind, but Chris was talking to Troy, the man who had more than one very good reason to detest Shane. Morbid curiosity kept him rooted to his chair and he continued to listen to the one side of the conversation he could hear.

"I'm in a coffee shop with a co-worker."

"His name?"

Shane shook his head in the hope of stopping Chris from mentioning him but Chris was looking at the table top and didn't notice.

"Shane, he's been..."

Chris was silent for long minutes while Shane wondered how much of the easygoing friendliness would be left by the time Troy stopped talking. When Chris lifted his gaze and studied him intensely it took all Shane had not to whither under the scrutiny.

"Listen, I'm finished here at five. I'll drop by Pins & Needles on my way home. We'll talk then. Shane said you'd have a story to tell me." Chris continued to stare at Shane as he listened for a few moments. "Okay, I'll see you later."

A deafening silence settled on the table when Chris put his phone away. Shane scrambled for something to say, but couldn't come up with anything except *told you so* and that would not only be childish but also make him more uncomfortable than he already was.

"Well," Chris said, "you clearly weren't joking when you told me Troy would want to tell me about you. From what he said and the way he said it I got the impression he doesn't like you very much."

Pent-up nerves got the better of Shane and a bitter snort escaped him. "He hates me. And if he doesn't, he should."

"That's very dramatic." A hesitant smile played on Chris' lips. "I can't imagine Troy hating anyone."

Shane was suddenly fed up with the whole situation. The thought that maybe he and Chris might be friends had been nice but he'd known it wasn't going to last. He might as well put an end to it all now. "Trust me, after he's told you the whole sorry tale you won't want to be around me anymore and I won't be able to blame you for that. I'll have a word with Barry when we get back and have him assign someone else to work with you next week."

"Hold on a minute, mate." The uncertainty had disappeared from Chris' face and was replaced by determination. "I'm inclined to make up my own mind about people. Sure, you and Troy have history and maybe it's ugly. Just because you two don't get on doesn't mean I can't like you. I work for Troy, he doesn't own my soul."

Shane checked the time, relieved to discover their lunch break was nearly over. "It's almost two. We'd better get back." He got up and walked to the exit without checking to see if Chris was following him. Before he was two steps away from the coffee shop Chris had caught up with him.

"I mean it. Don't say anything to Barry. If I, for whatever reason, feel I can't work with you anymore, I'll let him know." Chris fell silent for a moment. "Unless my connection to Troy makes you so uncomfortable that you can't stand to be around me. In that case, make whatever arrangements you feel necessary. Just don't do it on my behalf." A note of anger, or maybe it was frustration, had crept into Chris' voice.

Shane gave up the fight. After all, what difference did it make? Troy would tell Chris what Shane had done. Chances were that boyfriend of Troy's would throw in his two cents and Chris would at last realize Shane hadn't been exaggerating and be so disgusted with him he'd talk to Barry at the earliest opportunity. Shane couldn't allow himself to worry about it. There was too much going on in his world to add another burden. It would have been nice if the circumstances had been different. He would have liked to get to know this Australian man who was not at all his type and yet fascinated him, but it was not to be. It was a fact of life and Shane had learned that unless he accepted those, he'd drive himself crazy. He had to say something, though.

"Fair enough. I won't mention it again unless you do." He didn't add the words *it's been nice spending time with you* although they would have been true.

Chapter Four

Irritation and apprehension warred inside Chris when he walked through the door of Pins & Needles at half past five and he barely noticed the two men talking to Troy at the counter. He was convinced he'd seen the redhead and his dark-haired boyfriend before but couldn't be bothered trying to figure out when or where.

Damn it. He liked Shane. He'd liked him when they first met in the pub, and he'd been delighted when he'd discovered Shane would be supervising him while he worked for Barry. Sure, Shane had been standoffish after they'd gotten off together and he hadn't seemed too enthusiastic about seeing him in his workplace this morning, but by the time they'd gone to lunch they'd been getting along just fine. Fine enough for Chris to indulge in some mild flirting. Then the phone call from Troy had spoiled it all. The afternoon had been torturous. Chris had spent most of his time wondering what the hell the issue between Troy and Shane could possibly be and Shane had been preoccupied and withdrawn.

He waited while his boss finalized his dealings with the two cute young men, lost in his thoughts. A soft cough brought him back to present and he turned toward the sound to find Troy studying him from behind the counter. For the first time since he'd started working in Pins & Needles he wasn't entirely comfortable there.

"How're you doing?" Troy asked.

"Not too bad. And you?" Chris responded while he wondered why they were addressing each other as if they were strangers.

"Is Barry treating you all right? He can be an awkward bastard."

"Yeah, yeah. Everything is fine." The small talk nudged Chris' irritation up. "Are you done for the day? No more clients?"

"I am. You can lock the door for me, if you don't mind," Troy said. "Let's go to the back and have a beer."

Chris opened his mouth to point out that he hadn't come for a drinking session before swallowing the words. If whatever Troy was going to tell him was half as bad as Shane seemed to think, he could probably do with a beer or two while listening to it. He pushed the latch on the door, turned and followed Troy into the rooms where he used to live.

"Chris! It's good to see you." Xander stood in front of his drawing board, a pencil in his hand. "What do you think? Does it look like them?"

Troy and Chris walked closer to the board and studied the pencil drawing.

"Wow," Chris said, unable and unwilling to hide his admiration. "That is them. You managed to not only capture Eric and Lorcan's likeness but also who they are, their personalities. Right?" He turned to Troy, looking for confirmation.

"My boyfriend's a genius," Troy gushed before turning and giving Xander a quick and sweet kiss on his lips. "Chris is right," he said to Xander. "You've done it again. How you can express so much with what appear to be so few pencil lines is beyond me."

The blush creeping onto Xander's cheeks made Chris smile. The man was a celebrated artist and yet he still didn't believe in himself or his creations.

"I'll get us a drink." Xander didn't wait for an answer and rushed to the kitchen. Chris knew him well enough to know that while he needed the encouragement he didn't handle praise very well.

"Sit down." Troy nodded in the direction of the seating

area before taking the lead and sitting down on the couch.

Chris followed his employer and seated himself in an armchair opposite Troy. Suddenly tired and apprehensive again about what might be coming next, he rested his head against the back of his chair, closing his eyes for a moment. When he opened them and fixed his gaze on Troy he couldn't escape the impression that he was uncomfortable.

"Here you go." Xander joined them carrying three cans of lager and handed one to Chris before sitting next to Troy and giving him a beer too. "So, tell us, how was your day?" Xander stared at Chris expectantly.

"Never mind my day. It was fine." Chris knew he was being blunt but he had run out of patience. "I'd like to know what's going on with Shane. He's refused to say a word or even give me a hint. All I got from him was 'ask Troy' and 'this is Troy's story'. I'd really like to hear it now."

"That's all he said?" Troy looked and sounded surprised. "He didn't give you any details or make excuses?"

"Excuses for fucking what?" Chris squeezed his nails into his palms to try to keep a hold on his temper. After spending the whole afternoon imagining possible scenarios that had run from bad to ridiculous, he didn't want to play games.

Troy glanced at Xander for a moment, took a deep breath and turned to Chris. "I told you some of how I got to own this place, right?"

"Yes, you did. What has that got to...? Oh shit. That was *Shane*?" Chris felt as if someone had stuck a pin into him and all the air inside him was escaping. He remembered the story all too well. Troy had been in the process of opening a tattoo parlor with a colleague of his, only for the man to accept a job in Florida and leave at the last possible minute. By then Troy had purchased the equipment the shop needed and signed a five-year lease on the premises, meaning he'd had no choice but to own and run Pins & Needles on his own.

"There's more." Xander squirmed and glanced away

when he said the words.

"Do I want to know?" Chris asked, although he was fairly sure he wouldn't like hearing what he had to say.

"Probably not, but I think you should." Xander smiled apologetically. "It's not just that he left Troy in the worst possible lurch without a second thought." Xander stared at the coffee table and fiddled with his beer can. "He has" — Xander fidgeted — "*had* a habit of using people. Picking them up and dropping them as soon as they'd served his purpose. He did it to me before I met Troy and tried to do it again later, even after I told him I was with Troy. He just didn't care about other people or their feelings. It was all about him."

The words cut into Chris. He prided himself on being a good judge of character in general. His first impressions were rarely wrong and it had been a long time since he'd found himself forced to reassess an opinion he'd formed about anyone. Had he been wrong this time? Had he missed clues during his two encounters with Shane? Sure, the man had been dead set against exchanging contact details, but Chris had been under the impression that was the result of something in Shane's life rather than anything to do with Shane having used him. In fact, he'd picked Shane up that night in the pub, not the other way around.

He drained his can while thoughts continued to tumble through his head. Until this moment he'd thought Shane's standoffishness had nothing to do with Chris and everything to do with him working for Troy. *Damn it.* He'd liked Shane. He'd been thinking about ways to draw him out more, gain his trust and get to know him better. Could he still do that now he knew about everything that had happened in the past? Did his loyalty to Troy mean he had to reassess his impressions and change his attitude?

"You wouldn't have another tinny, would you?" Chris was suddenly sure one or two beers wouldn't do the trick for him tonight.

"Sure." Xander got up and headed for the kitchen while

Troy studied Chris.

"You look surprised."

"I am," Chris confirmed. "I didn't get a devious vibe off him at all. Insecure maybe. I thought he might be a bit of a loner. Everything you just told me on the other hand — it's a bit of a shocker."

"Well" — Troy shrugged — "you've only known him a day. I worked with him for years before I realized what a prick he was."

"Yes...well." Chris shut his mouth, suddenly unwilling to share the details of his previous encounter with Shane and afraid he'd already said too much.

"Oh?" Xander was back and handed Chris another beer. "Today wasn't the first time you met him?"

"I went out for a few drinks last night," Chris said while wondering why he felt the need to explain himself. "I met him in the pub. We had a..." He searched for the right words, "...an interesting encounter."

"And afterwards he treated you with disdain and stalked off." Xander didn't even try to make it sound like a question.

"No, actually." Chris could feel his temper rising. Just because Xander had had a bad experience didn't necessarily mean it would be the same for other people. "We had another beer together afterwards before going our separate ways. It wasn't until this morning..." He allowed the sentence to die off.

"He waited until you showed up in the parlor before he started treating you like shit?"

Chris bit on his tongue to stop himself from responding impulsively. He had to remember that he worked for these men who'd clearly both had very bad experiences with Shane. Just because he didn't have bad memories to look back on didn't mean Troy and Xander's feelings weren't valid. He glanced at the couple on the couch just as Troy lowered his hand to Xander's leg and flexed his fingers.

"Babe, it may seem unlikely, but it is not impossible Shane acted like a decent human being with Chris. I mean, it took

me three years before I found out what he was capable of."
Troy's voice was soft and soothing.

Xander visibly relaxed. "Yeah. I know that." He turned toward Chris. "I'm sorry. I'm rather touchy when it comes to Shane. He nearly ended our" — he pointed at Troy and himself — "relationship before it had a chance to begin. I still get upset every time I think about it."

"No! Really? You could have fooled me." Chris grinned and to his relief both Xander and Troy laughed along with him.

"Now I have a question." Chris said, focusing his attention on Troy who appeared to blanch somewhat under the sudden scrutiny. "Did you know I would be running into Shane?"

Embarrassment flashed across Troy's face. "Yes. Barry told me a few months ago that Shane had asked for his old job back and he'd given it to him."

"And you didn't give me a warning because...?" Chris was no longer angry. Only curiosity remained.

"I'm not entirely sure." Troy frowned, as if he was trying to work it out for himself. "I didn't want to send you there expecting the worst. I figured Shane wouldn't talk about it unless he was asked a direct question and if you didn't know you wouldn't broach the subject. I guess I hadn't figured on the possibility of the two of you meeting before today."

"Fair enough, I guess. I'm not sure a warning would have made much of a difference anyway," Chris admitted. "Even if you *had* told me I wouldn't have known he was the Shane you had told me about when I met him yesterday, so the situation would have been as awkward."

"How was it awkward? I mean for Shane maybe, but for you?" Troy asked.

"When he recognized me this morning he was convinced the whole thing had been a setup." Chris thought back to Shane's reaction earlier that day. "He was livid and it took a while before he believed that I really had had no idea who he was when we met and that I didn't know anything about any issues between you and him."

"You could have asked him." Xander snorted. "I'm sure he'd have been all too happy to give you some sort of half-truth version of events to make himself look better."

Chris' temper flared again. "You see, that's exactly what he didn't do. And not because I didn't press him for answers. All he said was that he wasn't Troy's favorite person and that Troy had good reasons for feeling that way. He kept on insisting that I ask you" — he switched his attention to Troy — "for the full story."

Chris waited for a reaction while Troy stared at some point on the wall, clearly lost in thought. "That doesn't sound like the Shane I know at all," he said at last.

Chris shrugged. "People are unpredictable." He concentrated on keeping his face blank. After all, he'd been grown up and living away from home by the time he found out how little he'd known about his mother. Not that Troy and Xander needed to know about that.

"So what does this all mean in practical terms?"

"What do you mean?" Xander and Troy asked at the same time.

"Now that you've told me all of this, what do you expect from me? Am I to keep my distance from Shane? Am I no longer going to be working there once a week?" Chris' frustration surfaced again. "Are you going to tell me how to live my life, who I can and can't hang out with?"

"Jaysus no!" Troy sounded and looked horrified. "I promised Barry we'd help him out, so we will. And I wouldn't dream of telling you how to pick your friends. I just figured you should know because...well, lots of reasons really. As you said, Shane already expected you to know. If I'd said nothing he would eventually have told you, and he's right about one thing — I did want to tell you this story myself." He thought for a moment. "I have a responsibility as your employer to not make your work more uncomfortable than it needs to be."

As he paused again, Chris pondered the strange formality in Troy's tone and choice of words. Not that he didn't agree that Troy had certain obligations toward him as his employer, but he'd thought the three of them had moved beyond having just a working relationship.

If the intensity of his gaze was anything to go by, Troy appeared to be trying to read Chris' expression. Then he smiled. "But most of all, as your friend it only feels right to warn you when I don't trust somebody you've met."

It should have been enough. Chris had been working for Troy for five months and over that time he'd come to like him. He enjoyed spending time with Xander and Troy. He'd only met Shane twice and the second encounter had been a rollercoaster of conflicting emotions to say the least. It shouldn't be a choice and yet... There was something about Shane that touched a place deep inside Chris. He had no idea why or what it meant but he couldn't get the man out of his head. The haunted expression occasionally flashing across Shane's features wouldn't leave him alone.

"So if I wanted to get to know Shane better that wouldn't be a problem? You two wouldn't be upset?" Chris swallowed hard, unsure whether or not he'd just taken a huge risk with a job he loved and two friends he didn't want to lose.

"Of course we wouldn't," Troy said before turning his head and looking at Xander, who smiled and nodded. Troy laughed. "We won't even say I told you so if he does end up letting you down. Just..." He studied the beer can in his hand for a moment before continuing. "Just don't bring him here for now. It would be awkward for all involved."

It took considerable effort for Chris to not deflate with relief. "I don't think he'd come here if I asked him." He lifted an eyebrow. "Now, are there any other skeletons hiding in cupboards that I need to know about?"

"Let me think." Xander grinned. "Did we ever tell you about the time we robbed the Bank of Ireland...?"

Tension fled the room as all three of them burst out laughing.

Chapter Five

Shane placed a bandage over the small tattoo he'd applied to the ankle of the young woman sitting in his chair and smiled up at his client. "There, you're all done. Just make sure to take good care of it and keep it clean. You can pay over at the counter." She got up and he watched her as she crossed the parlor while thinking about the story she'd told him about her tattoo. She'd picked the image of two drumsticks to commemorate her brother who'd died in a car accident four months ago, only twenty-two years old. It had been hard listening to her story and the pain in her voice as she related it—it cut too close to home.

"Shane, you may as well finish for today." Barry's voice pulled Shane back to the here and now.

"Are you sure?" he asked. "We're open for almost another hour."

"Go on." Barry's voice sounded gruff, as if he didn't want to be seen to be kind. "There's no other bookings for the day and the rest of us can deal with anybody who walks in between now and six."

"Thanks." Shane had no intention of questioning Barry again. He had more than enough to deal with right now and an extra hour in his day was very welcome. His mother wouldn't expect him until seven, which meant he could spend extra time with Ann before going home. As devastating as it was that she'd been moved to a hospice, it did mean he didn't have to worry about official and strictly guarded visiting hours any more. He hurriedly cleaned up his station and all but ran out of the door before Barry could change his mind.

The bus journey seemed to go on forever although it probably didn't take longer than twenty minutes. With nothing to keep him occupied, it was more than enough time for his thoughts to grow dark. He couldn't believe he was about to lose his sister. It just wasn't fair. She'd barely started her life at twenty-nine and it was all but over. He squeezed his eyes shut as he thought about Danny. The boy was only five and condemned to grow up without a clear memory of his mother, and whatever he would be able to recall would always be tinged with sadness. A deep sense of powerlessness settled on Shane, leaving him feeling fragile and insecure.

He opened his eyes again and saw he was nearing the stop where he needed to get off. Pushing his way through the other commuters, he made it to the front of the bus and jumped off as soon as the doors opened. He walked fast in an effort to outrun the thoughts tumbling through his head but it proved to be an exercise in futility.

He was scared. He'd never admit it out loud but thinking about the future petrified him. He'd always been in control of his life and had made a point of looking after number one. He knew it had gained him a reputation as a selfish bastard and he couldn't deny he'd always put himself first because he couldn't imagine someone else caring about him enough to do so. All he'd ever wanted was to live according to his own rules and until almost six months ago that was exactly what he'd done. Until that phone call. Until he'd had to come home from Florida. He couldn't have done anything else and still it felt as if life as he'd known it — as he'd imagined it would be — had ended that day.

"Hey, sis." He kept his voice low, all too aware that loud sounds, just as bright lights, physically hurt her. Then again, there was very little that didn't cause her pain these days.

"Shane, you're early." Her valiant attempt to smile at him broke his heart. Ann was the bravest person he knew and it wouldn't make a damn bit of difference to the outcome. Visiting her every day was slowly tearing him apart and the conversation he'd just had with her caregiver had done nothing to make him feel better, even if the news hadn't been unexpected. Ann seemed to disappear before his eyes, shrinking into nothingness. She was stick thin, her cheekbones so prominent they looked sharp enough to cut paper. Her eyes were dull, her gaze unfocused as a result of the pain medication she needed in ever-increasing quantities. He sat next to her bed and rested his hand on top of her blanket, leaving it up to her to decide whether or not she could bear to hold it.

"How's Danny?" she asked, and for a moment a light seemed to shine from her eyes.

"He's fine." Shane hesitated. He'd promised her he would never lie when she asked him about her son but telling her the full truth would only make her burden even heavier than it already was. "He's missing you of course but he's managing." *Just about. Except for the nightmares and the fact that he still doesn't understand that you won't be coming home again.* She didn't need to know those details. Shane had a feeling she sensed most of it anyway, but unless she came right out and asked him, he wouldn't tell her about Danny's panic attacks and nightmares. It wasn't as if she could do anything about them.

"I've signed him up for soccer. He's been showing a real interest and it will help keeping his mind off..."

"It helps him to think about something other than his dying mother." A sad smile appeared on Ann's face. "That's good. He's too young to have to deal with shit like this. I want him to be happy." She suddenly placed her hand on top of his and squeezed. "Remember that. He's only five. He doesn't need to grieve. I want you to allow him to laugh and enjoy himself, encourage him even. Don't let people tell him that he needs to be quiet or sad, not even Ma. Promise me."

Shane swallowed hard around the lump that had just formed in his throat. "I promise, princess. I'll do whatever I can to stop him from hurting, but he loves you. There's nothing I can do to prevent him from missing you."

"I know."

"And I don't want him to forget you." Shane cursed himself for the tears he could hear in his voice. The last thing Ann needed was to be burdened with his grief on top of all the pain and despair she had to be going through. "I'm going to make sure he'll always know what a truly remarkable and wonderful woman his mother was."

"I don't know." Ann looked troubled. "I've been thinking about that. I can't escape the feeling that it would be better for him if he just forgot me as soon as possible. If he doesn't remember me it won't hurt him as much."

Her words cut through him and Shane blinked hard to stop the tears from falling. "You're wrong. He'll want to know who he is and where he came from. Besides, he's five years old, there's no chance of him completely forgetting you. I just want to make sure he remembers all the good times and not just the sad ending."

Ann stared at him as silence settled in the room. He could almost hear her thoughts and knew she was weighing up the costs and benefits for Danny. It was almost impossible to figure out what the right thing to do might be so Shane had decided to follow his instincts. He had no doubt he would have wanted to know who his parents had been if they'd died when he was young. And while he thought about that...

"I know I've asked this before and how much you hate the question, but what about his father?"

"No!" For two short seconds the old Ann was back, all determined and fierce. "I told the prick when I found out I was pregnant and not only did he dump me, he disappeared from the face of the Earth." Anger flashed in her eyes before she deflated again. "I found him on Facebook shortly after I was diagnosed and contacted him. He basically told me he didn't care, that as far as he was concerned he didn't have a son, and since I had been stupid enough to have the child it was my problem. I do not want Danny to have to deal with that scum of the earth."

Shane was lost for words. For six long years Ann had refused to talk about Danny's father and why he wasn't around. He now understood her reasons and was almost sorry he'd pressed the issue. Except that he needed to know because one day Danny would demand the answers from him. The poor kid. What a way to start his life—a father who denied his existence and a mother who would be dead before he celebrated his sixth birthday.

"But I don't have to worry about that, do I, Shane?" The urgency in Ann's voice shocked him. "He'll have you. You'll raise him and support him for as long as he needs you, right?"

"Yes, princess." Shane forced his lips to stretch in what had to be a weak imitation of a smile. "I promised you I'd love and raise Danny and I will. I never meant that we should hand him over to his father. It's just that one day he'll be asking those questions and if I don't ask you now, I won't have any answers for him."

Ann closed her eyes and Shane thought she'd nodded off when she spoke again. "I know and I've thought about that. When it's all over..." She swallowed hard. "All Danny's paperwork will come to you—birth cert, inoculation records and the rest. There will also be an envelope containing the name of Danny's father. You're right. The boy is entitled to know even if the bastard doesn't deserve to have anything as beautiful as my boy in his life. But I need you to promise me something."

"Of course. Anything you ask." The words rushed out of Shane's mouth. He hated seeing his sister upset and he'd do whatever she wanted from him if at all possible.

"Don't you go and seek him out. I mean it. He knows about Danny and he knows I'm dying. If he wants to make contact he knows where to find my family. Right now I'm happy he's staying away. And the last thing anybody needs is you losing your temper and ending up facing an assault charge. Danny doesn't need more negativity in his life than he already has." She opened her eyes, lifted her head and glared at him.

His sister knew him well. The second she'd told Shane he would get the information he needed to find the bastard he'd decided he'd go and rip him a new one as soon as he got his hands on the paperwork. But she was right of course. He'd need to be strong and sensible for the boy. His days of acting impulsively were over. Messing up his own life was one thing – messing up Danny's would be unforgivable.

"I promise." He stared straight into his sister's eyes, wanting to show her he meant what he said. "I can't deny I'd love nothing more than to rearrange his face for him, but I won't do anything that might end up hurting Danny."

Ann closed her eyes again and rested her head against the pillows, suddenly looking even more exhausted than she normally did these days. "And don't tell him until he's at least sixteen years old and hopefully has the mental strength to deal with the information."

"Okay, sis. Anything you say. You're his mother, you decide." Shane could see she was fading fast and knew she'd be asleep before too long. "Do you want me to bring him for a visit on Sunday?"

A frown formed on Ann's forehead but she didn't open her eyes again. "Are you really sure that's a good idea? Every time Danny visits there's less of me left for him to remember. It must be so scary and confusing for him. His tears the last time he was here and had to leave..." She trailed off, clearly reliving the heartbreaking moment.

For a few seconds, Shane considered lying to his sister before deciding against it. "It isn't easy for him, I agree. But not seeing you would be even harder. It's the first thing he asks about every morning and the last thing he mentions before going to sleep – he lives for the times he can visit you, counts the days and marks them off on the calendar."

And he breaks my heart every single time. His sister didn't need that piece of information though.

"Okay. Yes. Do bring him." With what was clearly a

struggle she opened her eyes and gave Shane a faint smile. "I'd love to see him again next Sunday. Just send me a message before you leave the house so that I can try and make sure I'm not completely strung out on medication when you arrive."

"I will. Now go to sleep." He ached to stroke Ann's hair, take her in his arms and give her a long, comforting hug. The knowledge that both those actions would only make her more uncomfortable than she already was devastated him. He stayed in his chair, looking at his sister and memorizing her features, until he was sure she was fast asleep before getting up and leaving. He started running as soon as he'd left the hospice, sprinting as fast as he could in an effort to outrun the despair, to replace the pain in his heart with aching muscles and a sting in his side. When he reached the bus stop again he was too out of breath to cry, but his aching body did nothing to alleviate the breaking of his heart.

The unfairness of the whole situation enraged him. *What has my sister or Danny ever done to deserve this?* He stopped himself. He couldn't afford to indulge thoughts like that. He had to be strong, needed to keep on going. If it had just been him he'd have lost himself in a long string of alcoholic binges and one-nightstands just to forget about the whole nightmare. He wasn't on his own anymore though. His sister might still be alive but for all intents and purposes he already was Danny's carer and the boy deserved somebody he could depend on. He would have to be the man he'd never thought he might be and live a life he couldn't have imagined for himself in his wildest dreams — or nightmares for that matter.

And he'd be fucking good at it if it killed him. Besides, the one man he'd thought he could be really interested in appeared to have disappeared from his life. Four days had passed since he'd worked with Chris. He would have heard the full story from Troy by now. Since he hadn't been back to talk to him about it, Shane had to conclude that he'd been scared off.

That's probably just as well. It's not as if I have time to think about dating, never mind actually doing it.

Still, it would have been a nice fantasy to hang on to for a while. He could do with a break from reality and couldn't imagine one arising in his immediate future.

Chapter Six

Chris stopped walking when he reached his front door and put his shopping bags down, taking a moment to look at his house and count his blessings. It was something he did regularly. He never wanted to forget how lucky he'd been. When he'd arrived in Ireland ten years ago he'd thought he'd burned all his ships. If it hadn't been for his granny...

He entered the place he'd called home since the day after he'd arrived in Dublin and made his way to the kitchen to put his purchases away.

He'd always known his mother had moved from Ireland to Australia a few years before he was born. He'd always been curious about her past but before he'd reached his tenth birthday he'd learned not to ask her about it. It hadn't been until after his mother had died, when Chris was twenty-five, that he'd discovered he had a grandparent living in Dublin.

He glanced around the kitchen. Much had changed over the five years since his granny had died, leaving him truly alone in the world as well as in possession of the house they'd shared ever since he'd arrived from Sydney. With fresh paint on the walls in every room, all the carpets stripped, the wooden floors underneath brought back to life and the artwork purchased and hung on the walls by him, this house was truly his now. Most of the furniture, on the other hand, had been here when he'd first arrived and he had no intention of replacing any of it unless it fell apart. He liked living with the memories. He tried to hang on to every minute he'd spent with his grandmother as forcefully as he tried to forget about his life in Australia. His mother's eccentricity had ensured that he'd been the odd one out for as long as he could remember. When she'd rejected him as soon as he finished his schooling she'd effectively killed any bond there might have been between them.

He put the last of his groceries away, leaving just a pre-cooked lasagna on the counter and turned the oven on to heat it up.

He'd come to understand his mother's choices better as he'd grown up. In theory, he agreed that she should have been allowed to live her life exactly as she saw fit. In practice, her total disregard for rules, social graces and local customs had made the first eighteen years of his life a lonesome and hurtful time.

He opened the oven, put the pasta dish in and set the timer before grabbing a beer and walking into the living room where he collapsed on the couch, closing his eyes and allowing the memories to continue flowing through his mind.

The day after he'd graduated high school his mother had told him she'd be leaving. He'd been shocked when he discovered how well she had prepared for the moment she felt she could sever the ties between them. She'd made sure he wouldn't want for anything. The house he'd grown up in was mortgage-free and had been transferred into his name and there'd been an account with enough money to ensure he wouldn't need to go out and just take on any available job in order to survive.

He sighed. Seventeen years later, the only thing he still couldn't forgive her for was that she'd allowed him to believe he was alone in the world after she left. It wasn't until Chris had decided to sell the house and cleared out the attic that he'd discovered he did have a living relative in Ireland.

He picked up the remote control and flicked through the channels, not really seeing what flashed by on the screen. Not for the first time since his granny had died he considered renting out the spare bedroom in his house. Most of the time he enjoyed living on his own and not having to take other people's needs and demands into consideration— maybe he had more of his mother in him than he'd like to admit. But he'd never expected to spend his life on his own. As much as he loved his job and enjoyed the few hours he volunteered as a football trainer most weeks, they weren't enough to fulfill his dreams. He'd always assumed...

His mobile rang and he smiled when he saw the name on the display.

"I was just thinking about you." He smiled as he answered the call.

"You were? Nice thoughts I hope." Caroline, the woman he'd had a six-month-long relationship with shortly after he'd arrived in Dublin, laughed in response.

"Always nice thoughts," Chris answered.

"As it should be. But if that's the case, what's with the wistful tone to your voice?"

Damn the woman. She knows me too well.

"I was just reflecting that I didn't think I'd still be on my own by this stage of my life."

Caroline was quiet for a moment. "That's surprised me too," she admitted after a while. "You were born to be with someone, have a family." She fell silent again. "It just wasn't ever going to work out for us."

Chris sighed. It wasn't the first time they'd had this particular conversation. "More's the pity," he said in an effort to keep the conversation light.

"No, you're not getting off that easily. What has you all introspective all of the sudden? Don't tell me... You met someone."

Have I?

"I don't know," Chris replied. "I'm certainly interested for the first time in I don't know how long. But...it's complicated. And I barely know him, to be honest, and what I've heard about him isn't all that encouraging. But I can't get him out of my mind."

"Now I'm intrigued. We'll need to get together soon so you can tell me all about this man of yours."

The ease with which Caroline had accepted his bisexuality without question or suspicion from the moment they'd first met was one of the reasons he'd fallen for her years ago, and went a long way toward explaining why she was still his best friend.

"Ma, I'm hungry." A shrill voice sounded in his ear and Chris smiled ruefully as he imagined Maya, Caroline's four-year-old daughter, trying to get her mother's attention.

"Okay, that's my cue. Gotta go. How about I arrange for Peter to babysit tomorrow and we go for a drink and a catch-up?"

"Yes," Chris said, grinning broadly at the prospect. "I'd like that. Text me the time and place and I'll be there. Give my goddaughter a hug from me. Love you."

"Love you too."

As Chris pressed 'end call' the timer on his oven dinged, leaving him to reflect how uncanny it was that when it came to Caroline her timing always appeared to be spot on.

* * * *

"Now tell me all about this mystery person in your life." Caroline picked up her wineglass, took a sip and winked at him.

Chris smiled, surprised it had taken her a full thirty minutes before she asked the question. Then again, he'd allowed her to give him all the details about the latest developments in her daughter's life. Caroline was clearly still as in love with her little girl as she had been the day she was born and could talk about her forever.

"There's nothing to tell, really," Chris said. *If only there were.*

"You can't lie to me, Christopher. I know you too well. Come, give me all the scandal. It's your duty to bring some excitement to my domesticated lifestyle."

Scandal. He would have laughed if the word didn't cut too close to the truth.

"I promise you, there's not a lot to it. I met this man a week ago while I was out for a pint. We spent the evening together and I thought we got on fine but he refused to exchange numbers when the night was over, so I didn't think much more about it."

"But?" Caroline studied him. "There's more. Come on, give me the rest."

Chris sighed. He should of course have known she'd want the full story. "When I showed up in that parlor where I'm helping out for a few weeks the next day, he was there too. And it turns out he has history with Troy."

"Troy's your boss, right?" Caroline asked. "What sort of history? A relationship?"

"No, nothing like that as far as I know. But Shane did betray Troy in the worst sort of way. If I'd only heard about Shane without having met him I'd probably hate him and never give him a second look."

"Jeez, don't make me pull the story out of you sentence by sentence. Just spit it out because obviously you don't hate him."

"No, I don't. And I'm not sure why not." The question had been playing on Chris' mind ever since he'd left Pins & Needles that evening, almost a week ago. He liked and trusted Troy and Xander while he barely knew Shane. It shouldn't even have been a choice, and yet he couldn't get Shane out of his thoughts. "I just didn't get a devious vibe off him when we met. Somewhat of a loner was my first impression. And after we worked together I thought him defensive as well. But I don't know. I'm probably imagining things, but most of all I thought he seemed sad and tired."

He suddenly realized the story would only make sense to Caroline if he told it from start to finish, so that was what he did.

"If Troy and, what's his name, Xander, have no issue with you being friends with him, then what's the problem?"

Caroline asked, not unreasonably. "Did you talk to him since you last worked together?"

"No, I haven't seen or spoken to him."

"Hold on." Caroline looked incredulous. "He knew you would talk to Troy and told you that he expected you to dislike him after that conversation, and yet you didn't let him know you weren't about to turn your back on him? What's up with that?"

Fuck. Put in those terms, his decision to just let things lie for a week really didn't make any sense at all.

"It's not as if there's anything between us. He's the one who didn't want to exchange numbers. I figured going back to VikInk just to tell Shane Troy's story hadn't made me hate him, didn't feel appropriate. I'll see him tomorrow. We'll be working together again. We can talk then."

"Jaysus. By all that's holy, you men sure are fools." Caroline sounded disgusted. "Did it even occur to you that the only thing your six days of silence have probably achieved is to convince this Shane that he was right and you did end up taking Troy's side and now want nothing to do with him?"

"Yes, actually that thought did cross my mind. As did one that told me that searching him out only to tell him Troy's story hadn't changed anything might be too pushy." Chris frowned, suddenly fed up with the conversation. "It's too late now anyway. I'll see him again tomorrow, we'll see what happens then."

Caroline leaned back in her chair and visibly relaxed. "Okay. We'll drop the subject for now. It's just that I want you to be happy too, you know."

Chris' irritation evaporated. He knew only too well.

"You're not supposed to be on your own. I keep on saying this, but that's only because it's true. You were made to be in a relationship, to be part of a family. The only reason I'm pushing is because I don't want you to throw an opportunity away." She picked up her glass and drained the last few drops of wine. "Want another one?" She nodded at his

47

almost empty pint glass.

"Sure. Want me to get it?"

"No. My turn, and I need to take a detour first anyway."

Caroline picked up her bag and walked toward the toilets, Chris staring after her as memories flooded his mind. They'd connected the moment they'd first been introduced to each other and only a few weeks after meeting they'd been in a relationship. . They'd broken up, six months after their first kiss, not because they didn't get along but because they were too much like siblings. And that had never changed. Caroline was the sister he'd never had and the closest thing to family he'd had ever since his granny died.

"Penny for them." Caroline placed a pint of lager in front of Chris before sitting again.

"Nothing really." Chris smiled. "I was just thinking how happy I am that we're still friends."

"We'll always be friends." Caroline mock-glared at him. "And don't you forget it." She sipped from her glass. "So, what are you going to do next?"

"What do you mean? About what?" Chris had a pretty good idea what she meant but stalled on having to give an answer.

"About that Shane of yours."

Chris snorted. "He's hardly mine."

"Exactly. How are you going to change that?"

"Whoa, stop right there. What makes you think I want to change anything? Even if I thought he might be interested, which I don't, I'm not sure pursuing him would be a smart thing to do under the circumstances."

"Because the guy you work for told you to stay away from him?" Caroline's voice had a note to it, warning Chris that she'd be all over him if he didn't give the answer she wanted to hear.

"No. In fact, Troy hasn't told me anything like that. It just…well, if he'd been interested he would have exchanged numbers, wouldn't he? And to make a play for him when he may not be interested *and* he's in a long-running conflict with my boss just doesn't make a lot of sense."

"But you're attracted to him." It wasn't a question. Caroline knew him too well to have to ask.

"Yes, I am," Chris admitted. "It's been a while since I've felt this pull. But it doesn't really matter. I've got to work with him at least three more Thursdays. Pushing now will probably only make that more complicated than it needs to be." He shrugged.

Caroline said nothing, just studied him while sipping her wine, until he had to concentrate to keep himself from squirming in his chair. After what felt like minutes she nodded.

"Don't give up on the idea yet. I can tell you like him and you've been on your own for too long already. Chance it. Take a risk and see what happens next. You weren't meant to be alone." She leaned forward and lifted his hand from the table. "I've waited a long time to see you happy again. Don't make me wait longer than I have to." She laughed. "Or I may just start lining up blind dates for you."

He laughed along with her, not putting the possibility past her at all. And she was right—he'd never expected to still be on his own by this stage in his life. He'd always taken it for granted he'd end up with a partner and maybe even one or two children. It wasn't so much that his life was bad, it had more to do with knowing it could—and probably would—be better if he could share it with someone he loved, someone who loved him.

"I'll see what happens tomorrow," Chris said when he realized Caroline wasn't going to allow him to drop the subject until he'd somewhat reassured her. "If we're still on speaking terms by the end of the working day, I'll think again."

"Good boy." She winked and patted his hand before releasing it again. "And be sure to keep me informed about what follows."

"Yes, Ma." Chris smirked. "That's enough about me, thank you very much. What else is going on in your life?"

Caroline studied him for a moment before nodding and launching into a detailed and funny description of her routines. Chris picked up his pint, settled back in his chair and smiled when it only took her a few minutes before Maya became the sole focus of her story again. Not that he was surprised. The cute little girl had captured his heart too and had further strengthened the connection between him and Caroline. For the subsequent half hour all thoughts of relationships and attractive but confusing tattoo artists left his mind.

It wasn't until he was on his way back home, having put Caroline in a taxi first, that Shane pushed to the forefront of his mind again. *Maybe I should have talked to him before now.* If Shane had taken a week's worth of silence as proof that Chris had taken a dislike to him after his talk with Troy, Chris wouldn't be able to blame him. Since there was nothing he could do about the situation between now and tomorrow, Chris could only hope his rambling thoughts wouldn't keep him awake all night.

Chapter Seven

By the time Shane entered his sister's house he was ready to collapse. He knew he should have gone straight to his mother's place, next door, to pick Danny up, but he needed some time to unwind and prepare himself for the little boy's presence. As much as he adored his nephew, the few short months since he'd started looking after the lad—sharing the task with his mother—had not been enough for him to establish a rhythm that worked for him.

He collapsed onto the couch, rested his head against the cushions and closed his eyes. Just thirty minutes, then he'd relieve his mother who was no less exhausted than he was and doubtless getting ready to visit Ann in the hospice.

Ann. Every day he visited his sister, there seemed to be less of her. She was literally fading away in front of his eyes. The fact that he'd known how things would go once she'd been transferred from the hospital to live out her days in a place better equipped to deal with the dying didn't make it any easier for him.

Panic and anger churned in his stomach. This wasn't supposed to be his life. He hadn't signed up for this. In the past he'd always joked that one of the huge advantages of being gay was that he didn't have to worry about suddenly finding himself faced with fatherhood. And look at him now. The paperwork had all been signed. As soon as Ann died Danny would officially be his responsibility.

He opened his eyes and studied his surroundings. Nothing in this room or the rest of the house resembled anything he would have picked for himself. This was a family home rather than a bachelor pad. Where his personal style had been minimalistic bordering on sparse, he now lived surrounded by pretty ornaments and enough toys to fill a decent-sized shop. The thought brought a small smile to his face. He'd been responsible for quite a few of those playthings and stuffed animals. Spoiling Danny had always been easy and these days the temptation to just buy the lad new toys was even greater because it meant that for a few minutes at least he forgot how much he missed his mother.

Talking about mothers... Shane pushed himself up, walked out of his front door and knocked on the window of the neighboring house before letting himself in.

"Uncle Shane!"

He'd only just closed the front door behind him before Danny jumped into his arms. "Did you go and see Mammy? Did she ask for me? When can I see her?"

Shane hugged the boy as tightly as he could without hurting him while studying his mother, who'd followed Danny from the front room into the hall. She looked as tired as he felt and unlike him she wasn't in her twenties anymore.

"Are you okay, Ma? This little pest hasn't been bothering you too much, has he?" He tickled Danny before lowering him to the ground again, making the boy giggle.

"The boy's fine." Shane's mother smiled.

"Nanny made coddle for dinner," Danny said. "And I helped."

"You did?" Shane concentrated on Danny, knowing that he wouldn't be able to have a meaningful conversation with his mother as long as the boy was around. "What did you do?"

"I stirred, and that's the most important job because it all has to be mixed together well." Danny sounded very serious.

"So tonight's dinner is going to be extra special, is it?"

Danny nodded enthusiastically. "I already had mine and it was sooooo good."

Shane glanced at his mother, who shrugged.

"He was hungry so we ate early. I'm sorta glad. It means I can go and see Ann a bit earlier tonight. There's a plate for you in the microwave. You just need to heat it up."

"Thanks, Ma." The words didn't feel like enough. His mother's life had been turned on its head just as Shane's had. As much as she loved her only grandchild, she'd never thought she'd be caring for Danny five days a week while Shane worked. She'd all but given up on any social activities she'd been engaged in before Ann had gotten ill.

"Nanny?" Danny turned to his grandmother, tilted his head and Shane didn't need to see his face to know the boy's eyes would be spread wide. "Can I come with you? I wanna see Mummy too." A soft whine crept into Danny's voice.

"Not tonight, buster," Shane said, sparing his mother the ordeal of having to refuse the lad. "You've seen her last weekend and we'll go again next Sunday. And that gives you loads of time to draw a new picture for her. Have you decided what it's going to be yet?"

Danny's lip wobbled before he pulled himself together.

"Our house?" Danny asked. "She can look at it and remember to hurry up and get better so she can come back."

Watching the boy struggle to control his emotions was harder than seeing him cry or calming him down after his frequent nightmares. No child so young should have to try to get his head around losing his only parent. Five year olds weren't supposed to understand the concept of death or forever.

"You go on, Ma. I'll have my dinner and then Danny and I'll move next door. Why don't you drop in for a cuppa on your way home?"

"I'll do that. Thanks, son." She turned to Danny. "Come here and give your nanny a big hug so I can carry it with me and pass it to your mammy."

Danny did as he was told. "Will you ask her when she's coming home? Tell her I miss her." Danny's voice was thick with the tears he stubbornly tried to hold back.

The despair in his mother's eyes when she glanced up at him tore at Shane. They'd tried to explain to Danny that his mother wouldn't be coming home, but the boy had no concept of what death was. He was too young to understand that forever was longer than the time between one Christmas and the next.

After giving her grandson one last kiss, Shane's mother pushed herself up, grabbed her cardigan from the hook next to the door and let herself out.

"Now you'd better show me this extra special dinner you cooked for me, lad."

Thanks be to God for five year olds and their short attention spans. Danny's face lit up as he took Shane's hand and pulled him to the kitchen, clearly excited to show him the dinner he'd helped to prepare.

* * * *

Two hours later Danny had been bathed and was fast asleep. He'd only needed to have two stories read to him before he couldn't keep his eyes open any longer. Shane tiptoed his way out of Danny's room, softly closing the door behind him while sending up a silent prayer that the boy would for once have a peaceful night's sleep.

Shane entered his kitchen, opened the fridge and stared longingly at the cans of beer before closing the door again and filling the kettle with water. His mother wouldn't be much longer and he'd promised her a cuppa. Besides, beer, or rather any form of alcohol, only appeared to make him feel worse rather than better. He'd tried drinking himself into oblivion when he'd first arrived home. Much to his disgust he'd discovered that being drunk didn't stop his worries, his grief or his pain at the prospect of losing his sister. Quite the opposite really—it turned his thoughts even darker than they normally were.

The boiling kettle switched itself off at the same time as his doorbell rang. Shane shook his head. He'd no idea why his mother didn't just use the key she had. If he could just waltz into her house, why didn't she do the same here?

He opened the door determined to tell her once again to let herself in, but one look at his mother's face had him swallowing the words and opening his arms.

"You could have warned me," she muttered into his shoulder as he hugged her tightly.

"Not in front of Danny I couldn't," Shane replied. "The boy has it hard enough because we won't allow him to visit more than once a week. He's worried sick without having to see what we encounter every day. I'm not going to make it even more difficult for him with careless words." He swallowed. "I'm sorry, Ma. Today was a very bad day for our girl."

His mother straightened and extracted herself from his arms. "And it's only going to get worse. I know this. You know it. And still it shocks me to see how fast she's deteriorating from one day to the next." She gazed at him, her expression exhausted and tear-filled, before she visibly shook herself. "Now, what was that about a cup of tea?"

Shane watched as his mother sat on the couch, resting her head against the cushion and closing her eyes just as he'd done only a few hours earlier, before he walked into the kitchen area of the open plan ground floor and switched the kettle back on.

A few minutes later, when he turned with two mugs of tea in his hands, he thought she might have dozed off but she blinked her eyes open as he put the cups on the table.

For a few minutes they sipped their hot drink in silence, taking comfort in each other's presence without the need for words.

"We don't have much more time left." His mother put her empty mug back on the table, making sure to avoid looking Shane in the eyes as she did so.

"I know." Shane sighed. "I spoke to her caregiver before I saw Ann. She reckons two weeks tops." He wished he knew how to keep the tears from thickening his voice, but if such a thing were possible he'd yet to discover how.

His mother nodded, tears swelling in her eyes before trickling down her cheeks.

"I feel so selfish for wishing we could keep her just a little while longer. It breaks my heart to see my baby girl in so much pain and yet I can't bear the thought of losing her, even if I do know that will be an end to her suffering."

"I know, Ma. I feel the same. I want her to be free of pain but I can't imagine going on without her. I dread the day I'll have to tell Danny his mammy is gone although by this stage I can't help feeling that might be easier on the lad than this situation is."

"There are no easy answers, and life will only get harder over the foreseeable future." His ma visibly pulled herself together. "But we've had this discussion before. That's not what I wanted to talk about."

"Okay." Shane tried to keep the nerves suddenly dancing through his belly out of his voice. "What's up?"

"I'm worried about you," she said. "You look like death on legs, as if you might collapse at any moment. When was the last time you had a full night's sleep?"

This turn in the conversation was unexpected, to put it mildly. He'd been worried caring for Danny five days per week might be getting too much for his mother. He could see how tired she was and if he had any other options he'd use them. Shane didn't want to get a virtual stranger to come and mind Danny while he worked — the boy's life was unsettled enough as it was. He couldn't afford to work less either, even if he thought Barry would be open to such a suggestion. His mother had no business worrying about him. He was no more tired than she was.

"Ma, stop it." He kept his voice soft while also trying to make it clear that he was having none of this nonsense. "Have you looked in the mirror recently? You're not looking too well-rested yourself."

"But at least I get my eight hours every night." She sighed. "Answer my question, when was the last time your sleep wasn't interrupted? Can you even remember?"

"I don't know." Shane thought for a moment and realized he really didn't have any idea. "It doesn't matter. Danny needs me when he wakes up scared."

"I know. And you've no idea how grateful I am you're here. I couldn't have done this on my own." His mother stared at him for a moment. "But you need a break. You've been making sure I have at least one child-free day every week ever since you came home. I think it's time you had some time to yourself."

"Ma, there's no need. Like you said, it won't be much longer. I'll keep going for as long as I need to."

His mother reached for his hand and squeezed it. "I know, love. And I appreciate it, but you are going to need your strength more than ever after Ann dies." She swallowed hard. "I've talked to Ann and told her that I'll be taking Danny to Bettystown from tomorrow to Sunday. Peggy has invited me to stay with her for a few days. The weather is supposed to stay nice and it will do Danny the world of good to play on the beach. We'll come back on Sunday. Peggy has promised to drop us off at the hospice."

Shane opened his mouth to object but before he could voice his concerns, she continued.

"I feel bad about going away now that Ann is so close to…" She paused, blinking hard. "But we discussed it and Ann agrees with me that those few days are just what you and Danny need. And if anything were to happen, we'll be less than an hour away from the hospice."

All the arguments against his mother taking the young boy away died on Shane's lips as soon as she mentioned Danny being able to enjoy the seaside. If it distracted the lad from the misery in his life for a day or two, who was Shane to put up barriers?

"Are you sure, Ma? I don't have to tell you he can be a handful."

"No, you don't have to remind me. But remember. I managed to raise both you and Ann just fine and it's not so long ago I've forgotten how to do it. Besides, there'll be two of us there. You know Peggy. She adores Danny. The only risk we're taking is him being spoiled rotten."

Shane laughed. "Spoiled even more than we already do, you mean."

The smile on his mother's face, fleeting as it was, warmed Shane's heart.

"That's settled then," she said. "Peggy will be picking us up around ten tomorrow morning. Don't worry about packing for the lad. I'll deal with that after you've gone to work."

"Okay. Yes, it will be good for Danny."

"And for you," his mother insisted, because she had to have the last word, as she always did.

Chapter Eight

Chris took a deep breath and pulled open the door to VikInk. He didn't know whether to laugh at himself or to be disgusted. He couldn't remember the last time he'd been nervous about having to meet someone, but this morning he'd woken up with a tense feeling all through his body. He knew he was being silly and yet, no matter how often he told himself he had nothing to worry about, he couldn't stop the nerves from swirling through his belly.

He glanced through the parlor and saw Barry behind the reception desk.

"Morning," Barry said, glancing up at him.

"Howya. Same deal as last week?" Chris wasn't sure what he wanted the answer to be.

"Yeah. You work with Shane again. It went well enough last week. Here, I wrote you out a list of your appointments for today." Barry pushed a piece of paper across to counter.

Chris studied the list for a moment, noting that he'd once again been given small and relatively simple jobs to deal with. It made sense of course. He only worked here one day a week and even that was temporary, but it didn't make for a varied working day.

"Shane isn't here yet but he shouldn't be much longer. Help yourself to a cup of coffee before setting up where you were working last week. Your first appointment isn't for another half hour or so."

"Sure. Thanks." Chris turned and walked to the small kitchen, looking forward to a large mug of coffee and a few minutes to compose himself before he'd be face-to-face with Shane.

While he poured himself a cup, he wondered again whether he should have tried to contact Shane after he'd had his conversation with Troy and Xander last week. Shane had been convinced Chris wouldn't want to be anywhere near him after he'd heard the full story about his history with Troy. And to be fair, Chris could understand why he'd thought that. Of all the shitty things a person could do, Shane had certainly pushed all limits. It wouldn't be surprising if he'd interpreted Chris' lack of contact over the past seven days as confirmation of that conviction.

His first sip of coffee felt like heaven and he drank the much-needed caffeine as fast as he could, given the temperature of his beverage.

Of course, his reasons for not reaching out to Shane had had nothing to do with what had happened in the past. Chris just hadn't been sure contacting Shane just to reassure him would be appropriate. They barely knew each other. They'd had one encounter on a night out and had worked together for a single day. Neither of those made them friends, never mind anything more than that. And yet...

"Morning."

The greeting sounded both gruff and hesitant while the voice sent a little shiver down Chris' spine. He took a deep breath, plastered a smile on his face and turned toward the entrance to the small kitchen.

"Hey. Ready to supervise me for another day?"

Keeping his expression relaxed and happy while he studied Shane was hard. He looked exhausted with dark smudges underneath his eyes and deep frown lines on his forehead.

"I guess so," Shane replied. "I have to say you surprised me. I was convinced you would have asked Barry to place you with someone else."

"Now why would I do that?" Chris asked. "We worked well together last week and I see no reason why we shouldn't do the same today."

"You didn't talk to Troy about me then." The certainty in

Shane's voice was totally understandable and yet it shocked Chris.

"I did. I spoke with Troy and with Xander. You were right. What they told me didn't paint a flattering picture of you."

An utterly confused expression flashed across Shane's features before he turned away and approached the coffee machine. "And yet here you are saying you're happy to work with me." Shane focused on pouring himself a cup of the black stuff. "Maybe I'm being thick, but I don't get it."

Chris checked the time before answering.

"My first appointment will be here in a minute, so maybe we could have lunch together again and talk then?"

Shane turned back with both his hands clasped around his mug, studiously not looking at Chris. "Sure, we can do that. If you're sure that's what you want. Like I said last week, I'd completely understand if you want nothing more to do with me."

Chris walked past Shane and rinsed his mug at the sink before placing it on the draining board. "I'm my own man." He kept his voice soft and friendly. "Even if Troy had told me to stay away from you, it would have been my decision in the end." He turned and faced Shane who stared at him with a combination of confusion and hope shining from his eyes.

"You're telling me he didn't warn you about me?"

Chris smiled. "We'll talk over lunch. I've got work to do."

* * * *

Almost four hours and several small tattoos later, Chris led the way out of the parlor as he and Shane started their break. Chris had been fully aware of Shane studying him on and off all through the morning. Maybe it hadn't been fair to leave him hanging like that, but the conversation they were about to have wasn't one he wanted to conduct where all of Shane's colleagues could overhear them and he couldn't imagine Shane wanting a public discussion about his past behavior either. Now that he was only minutes away from explaining what he didn't quite understand himself, nerves cramped his stomach and he wasn't sure how much, if anything, he'd be able to eat.

They strolled in silence to the same coffee shop they'd used a week earlier. Chris gazed straight ahead, ignoring the urge to study Shane. Everything would be so much easier if he could just understand how this man had managed to get under his skin in so little time. As it was Chris couldn't shake the feeling there was a lot more to Shane than what he'd been told by Troy and Xander, and if he had anything to say about it, he would discover exactly what that was.

They went through the routine of ordering, paying and finding an empty table before Shane's patience broke.

"Are you going to put me out of my misery now?"

Shane's question sounded full of bravado, as if it didn't matter what Chris might say, but his pinched expression belied his tone of voice.

"Okay, here goes." Chris thought for a moment before deciding that simple honesty was the best way to go. "You told me to talk to Troy and that's exactly what I did." He picked up his glass and had a long drink of water before continuing. "I'd heard the story before. I knew Troy was supposed to have a partner when he opened Pins & Needles and that this person had done a runner shortly before the place opened. I just didn't make the connection when I met you."

"But now you do. And you're still here having lunch with me?" Shane threw in the question before Chris had a chance to start his next sentence.

"Very perceptive of you," Chris joked before turning serious again. "Listen, it's not rocket science. It has been a long time since I've allowed anybody else to tell me how to live my life or how to pick my friends. Sure, it was a bastardly thing to do, leaving Troy in the lurch like that. Not to mention the stunt you pulled later, when he and

Xander ran into you in that club. But it has nothing to do with me. I like Troy, I love working for him and I would hate to lose that job, but none of that means that he's now got the right to run my life for me."

"Then Troy did tell you to stay away from me." Shane sounded almost relieved to have reached the conclusion.

"No, he didn't actually. He..." Chris tried to find a diplomatic way of repeating what Troy had said before deciding again that honesty was probably the best way to go. It wasn't as if Shane wouldn't expect the worst. "He told me that he'd never tell me how to live my life or who to spend my time with but that he wouldn't be my friend if he didn't warn me."

"Oh." Shane picked up his sandwich, studied it and put it back on the plate. "I wish I could say that surprised me." He looked up and stared straight into Chris' eyes as if he wanted to reassure him of his honesty. "But it doesn't. Not really. I wouldn't have blamed him for telling you to stay well away from me, but I should have known. Troy always was a better man than that." He lowered his voice and Chris had to strain to hear his last words over the noise from the other people chatting around them.

"A better man than me."

Chris was lost for words. What could he say? He didn't know Shane well enough to dispute that statement. And yet the questioning expression on Shane's face made it perfectly clear he was waiting for some sort of response.

"I've no way of knowing that." Chris opted for honesty once more. "Like I said to Troy, I prefer to make up my own mind about the people in my life." He hesitated for a moment, wondering how frank he should be, before deciding that half-truths wouldn't help anybody right now. "I'm a big boy." He grinned, hoping to lighten the mood at least a little. "So far you've given me no reason to think you're a bastard." He shrugged. "We'll see what happens next."

Shane picked up his sandwich again and took a bite. He

chewed slowly, almost as if he wanted his mouth to be full so he couldn't be expected to talk. Chris followed his example, suddenly hungry now the conversation he had dreaded appeared to be behind him. They ate in silence while Shane studiously looked at anything except Chris, making him wonder what was going on in his head. He'd told Shane they'd see what happened next without having a clear idea what form any possible 'next' might take. He knew what he wanted. But he wasn't at all convinced Shane would be interested in going to the pub together.

The second half of his sandwich tasted like cardboard as Chris realized that while he'd certainly hoped that once he'd talked to Shane the two of them would be on their way to getting to know each other better, it was more than likely that Shane had only been worried about whether or not his past would catch up with him. Just because Chris couldn't keep Shane out of his thoughts didn't mean he felt the same. After all, Shane had refused to exchange contact information even before he'd found out who Chris worked for.

He put the remainder of his lunch back on his plate and pushed it to the middle of the table. He'd probably regret it later on but he couldn't make himself eat any more.

"What's that supposed to mean?" Shane sounded almost antagonistic.

"Excuse me?"

"You said, 'We'll see what happens next'. Why do you think anything would happen?"

"Oh." *Fuck.* "I didn't really mean anything." *Nothing I want to suggest out loud if you're going to be this defensive anyway.* "Just that there's absolutely no reason to ask Barry to find me someone else to work alongside, or for us to stop having lunch together."

Shane studied him, his face scrunched up, as if he wanted to ascertain whether or not Chris was telling the truth.

Suddenly he was fed up with the whole circus. "Listen, if it makes you uncomfortable that I normally work for

Troy, by all means ask Barry to put me somewhere else. For fuck sake. All I'm trying to say is that what happened between you and Troy or even you and Xander in the past has nothing to do with me. I think I'm old enough to make up my own mind about the people in my life. But hey, you do what you think is best. I'm only supposed to work in VikInk for another two days so it really doesn't make that much of a difference."

Something flashed in Shane's eyes before he averted his gaze and picked up his coffee. He'd had enough of this. Maybe his first impression had been wrong after all. Just because it didn't happen often didn't mean he was incapable of misjudging people. He drained his cup and pushed his chair back.

"I'm going for a walk before we need to start again."

"Wait."

Chris was halfway out of his chair when Shane's voice stopped him.

"I'm sorry. I was so sure Troy would warn you away from me, or even if he didn't, that our history would mean you'd rather not be anywhere near me..." Shane gazed up at Chris. "I guess part of me is still waiting for the axe to fall."

Chris sat back down, wondering why he couldn't make himself leave. What was it about Shane that made it impossible to just say 'fuck it' and forget about him? He almost laughed at himself — as if he didn't know. He was a sucker for that expression Shane sported on his face right now, signaling something between hope and disbelief. He was certain there was more going on than just the Pins &Needles drama and, fool that he was, Chris wanted to know the full story.

"Okay. If you're sure." He studied Shane. "If this is only because you're afraid of upsetting Barry you can forget about it, though. The next time you start this debate up again I'm gone." He knew he was glaring at Shane but he wanted to get his message across. "You can either accept what I'm saying or not. No skin off my nose. But you have to stop this trying to second guess me." He took a deep breath and relaxed some. "I'm a simple person, really. If I ever do get fed up with you, you'll know about it. But it would be for my own reasons, not somebody else's."

"Fair enough." A tenuous smile tugged at Shane's lips. "I'll shut up about it now. It's been fun working with you so far and I wouldn't mind keeping it up."

"Good." Chris looked at the food counter and grinned. "Now that we've got that settled, how about a treat? Apple pie or cheesecake?"

Surprise flashed across Shane's features, immediately followed by a smile. "Apple pie, hot with lots of cream, please."

"Great minds…" Chris got up and approached the counter, wondering why he was prepared to put up with all this hard work for a man who'd shown no real interest in him since their hook-up. *Am I just that desperate or is there really something here?*

Chapter Nine

What am I doing here?

Shane stopped walking and stared at the door. *What the fuck possessed me to say yes?*

Of course it had made perfect sense two hours ago, when he and Chris had left VikInk together rafter a relaxed afternoon's work ended.

'Have you got plans for tonight?' Chris had asked the question in a tone that suggested the answer didn't matter. His inability to look Shane in the face told a different story.

'Not really,' Shane had answered as soon as he realized that there wouldn't be a small boy and a tired mother waiting for him by the time he made it back home. 'I'll have to be somewhere for the next hour or so, but after that I'm a free man for the first time in ages.' The words had slipped from his mouth before he could think better of it and he saw the quizzical expression on Chris' face as soon as he stopped talking.

Don't ask me to explain. Please don't ask me to explain. *The words screaming in his head must have been visible in his expression because Chris had studied him, opened his mouth and closed it again before nodding.*

'Wanna come to my place for a spot of dinner?'

There'd been so many good reasons to say no. He didn't have time to even think about getting involved with anyone. He'd probably be lousy company after he'd visited Ann. Shane didn't want to answer the questions Chris might have once they started talking about themselves to each other. There was also one very compelling reason to say yes – he didn't want to go back to his sister's house where everything would continue to remind him of the nightmare his life had turned into without having Danny around to keep him busy and distracted.

'Sure.'

Less than five meters separated Shane from Chris' front door but he couldn't make his feet move. Why *had* he said yes? He felt empty, drained after his visit to the hospice. He wasn't sure how Ann was still alive. Her skin appeared transparent and she barely took up any space in her bed. Her carer had told him again that she might have only weeks left. One look at her had convinced him that days was a more realistic expectation.

"Would you like me to serve you your dinner there or are you coming in?"

Shane blinked hard. He'd been so lost in his dark musings he hadn't seen the door open, hadn't been aware of Chris standing there waiting for him to make a move.

"Sorry." He forced a laugh. "Got caught up in my thoughts, I guess." His feet felt heavy as he took the last few steps separating him from Chris. "I hope I'm not late?"

He hadn't stayed with Ann very long. She hadn't woken up while he was in her room and after half an hour of listening to her labored breathing he'd written her a note and left again. He'd walked the three miles from the hospice to Chris' house in the hope it would clear his head and put him in the right frame of mind to be sociable, but obviously it hadn't worked.

"We don't have to do this, you know?"

Shane stopped in front of Chris and studied his face, expecting to find frustration or impatience but only seeing concern.

"I mean," Chris continued. "If you'd rather not spend time with me, that's okay. Just say the word."

Shane felt like a heel. He probably shouldn't have accepted the invitation. He just didn't have it in him to be good company to anyone right now. But he had said yes, so the least he could do was make an effort. Besides, he didn't dread an awkward evening anywhere near as much as he feared being alone with his thoughts.

"What?" he smirked. "Did you ruin our dinner? Are you looking for an excuse not to feed me?"

Chris studied him for a moment, obviously not convinced by his attempt at lighthearted humor, before relaxing.

"I'll have you know I'm a pretty good cook." He stepped back from the threshold. "Come in and find out."

Shane followed Chris into the house and down a narrow hallway to the kitchen, relieved he had apparently managed to steer the situation away from inner turmoil. His mother was right—he did need a distraction from the constant battle his life had turned into. There was no reason why he couldn't try to push Ann and Danny to the back of his mind while he enjoyed himself for just one evening. Especially since it wouldn't be long before it all went to Hell.

The kitchen wasn't very big or stylish but did give off a comfortable, homey vibe he liked. The wooden cabinets and table and chairs contrasted nicely with the blue tiles. A chopping board loaded with vegetables on one side and chicken pieces on the other sat next to the cooker on top of which a pot of water boiled softly, the bubbles blending in with music Shane didn't recognize playing in the background.

"Hungry?" Chris asked.

"Starving," Shane said, surprised to discover it was actually true.

"Good." Chris grinned. "Oh, you're not allergic to nuts, are you?"

"No, as far as I know I'm not allergic to anything. I *am* curious as to what you'll be feeding me now."

"Does chicken satay stir fry sound okay to you?"

"Sure, don't think I've ever had that before but if those" — Shane pointed at the chopping board — "are the ingredients, there's no reason I wouldn't like it."

"Good." Chris opened a cabinet and extracted a wok which he placed on the cooker before turning it on to its highest setting. "Help yourself to a drink. There should be something you'll like in the fridge." He nodded to his left where a large fridge-freezer took up more than its fair share of space.

Shane laughed out loud when he looked at the wide selection of soft drinks and alcoholic beverages. "Are you running a secret pub here?"

Chris finished pouring oil into the wok before turning to Shane with a somewhat sheepish expression. "Nah, I just like having a choice."

"You want something?" Shane helped himself to a can of cider while he waited for Chris' response.

"Sure, I'll have a Heineken. Could you pass me the plastic container too?"

"With the brown stuff in it?" Shane studied the dish in his hand suspiciously.

Chris laughed. "That's the satay sauce." He held out his hand and took both the sauce and the can from Shane. "Sit down." He nodded in the direction of the table. "This won't take long."

Chris dropped the chicken pieces into the wok and stirred them around. He was remarkably graceful given how big he was and the limited space in the kitchen. He swung his hips in time with the music playing from speakers Shane couldn't see.

"What are we listening to?"

"The Gotan Project." Chris took a pack of noodles from an overhead cabinet and emptied it into the pot of boiling water. "Do you know them?"

"Never heard of them," Shane said. "But I like what I'm hearing."

"Cool." Chris glanced over his shoulder, smiling, before turning back to the cooker and adding the selection of vegetables and mushrooms to the chicken pieces.

"Anything I can do?" Shane asked.

"No, you're good. Just sit and relax. I've got this." Chris opened the container and spooned about half its contents into the pan, added some water from the noodle pot and stirred.

The kitchen filled with a wonderful aroma. The combination of fried onion, garlic, chicken and something spicier Shane couldn't identify made his mouth water and, moments later, his stomach grumble.

In a few fluid movements Chris drained the noodles, added them to the wok and used a pair of tongs to mix the ingredients up. "That should do it." He grabbed two plates from a cabinet and filled them with generous helpings of the delicious-smelling concoction. "Here you go." He passed a plate to Shane. "I hope you'll like it."

"If it tastes as good as it smells…"

Shane took a tentative forkful of food and almost groaned out loud. "This is bleeding wonderful." He tried to identify the individual flavors on his tongue. There was chicken, of course, and spring onion and garlic as well as peanuts and what he thought had to be soy sauce. There was a delicious hot after-kick as soon as he swallowed his first bite so he figured there had to be something like hot peppers in there as well.

He stopped trying to dissect his dinner and just enjoyed it. He'd been living off meals cooked by his mother or brought home from the chipper for the past few months and hadn't realized how much he'd missed more exotic tastes. While he lived in Florida he'd indulged in eating foods he wasn't familiar with, discovering new favorites every day. Ever since he'd come home it had been the standard meat and two veg. Not that there was anything wrong with that—his mother was a good cook and he was grateful she prepared dinner for him and Danny more evenings than not—but it had all been very plain and equally predictable.

When his plate was empty—and all but licked clean—Shane leaned back in his chair and looked at Chris who returned his stare, amusement shining from his eyes.

"No complaints about my cooking then?"

"Fuck no. That was great. I don't suppose…?"

Chris grinned. "Yes, there is more." He stood, got the wok from the cooker and upended it over Shane's plate.

"On you go."

* * * *

"That was amazing." Shane put his fork on his once again empty plate. "I'm stuffed. Excuse me while I..." He opened the button on his suddenly very tight jeans before turning his attention to Chris, just in time to see something resembling heat flash in his eyes.

Shit. What message am I sending out? Do I even want to go there?"

"Where do you get your hands on that sauce?" he asked, both because he wanted to know and to deflect attention from his partially opened trousers.

"You can't get it here as far as I know," Chris answered. "Not like that, anyway. I make it myself. A Dutch friend gave me the recipe years ago, when I still lived in Australia. I'll write it out for you if you're interested."

For a moment Shane wondered whether or not he'd get Danny to eat a dish like the one he'd just enjoyed, before realizing that the only way to find out was to put it in front of the kid. "Yeah, if you don't mind. I can do with some variation in my diet."

"No worries, mate. Remind me before you go."

Relief and disappointment flooded Shane. It was good to know there were no expectations on Chris' part but on the other hand Shane couldn't deny he'd hoped the invitation had come as a result of attraction. He wouldn't mind a repeat of the evening they'd spent together two weeks ago.

He lowered his gaze as Chris picked up the plates and put them in the sink. He was being stupid. What they'd done that night had been nothing more and nothing less than an encounter, a meaningless hook-up. And that was how it should be, how it had to be. He didn't have time or the emotional wherewithal to cope with anything beyond casual right now.

"What did that table ever do to you?" Chris' voice

sounded strained when it broke through Shane's thoughts. "What?"

"You're frowning at my furniture as if it's upset you."

"Oh. Sorry. It's nothing." Shane hoped it would be enough but knew he had to stop losing himself in his thoughts unless he wanted Chris to start asking questions he had no intention of answering.

"How long have you been in Ireland then?"

Chris blinked at Shane as if surprised by the sudden shift before replying. "Ten years."

"You go back a lot?"

A frown flashed across Chris' face. "I haven't been back since I got here. There's nothing to go back to or for."

Questions burned on Shane's lips but he stopped himself from asking. He had no intention of talking about what was going on in his own life so it wouldn't be fair to ask Chris for details about his.

Chris sighed. "It's no big secret. My mother more or less abandoned me when I was eighteen. I stayed in Sydney for another seven years. After she died I discovered I had a granny in Ireland my mother had never told me about. I came to visit and just never went back." Chris sounded matter of fact but the clipped voice told a different story.

"That sucks." Shane said. "Why did she kick you out? Because you're gay?"

Chris said nothing.

"Shit, I'm sorry. It's none of my business. Forget I asked." Shane wished he'd kept his big mouth shut. He should have stuck to his first plan and kept his questions to himself.

Chris shrugged. "It's cool. No, it had nothing to do with that. In fact, I'm bi, not gay. But that didn't play a role either. She just didn't like being a mother and figured she'd done enough as soon as I was legally an adult." He paused for a moment. "Not that she was a bad parent before then. She wasn't very affectionate, but I never lacked anything." He laughed, the sound harsh rather than happy. "In fact, I was blissfully unaware she resented having to look after me until she stopped doing it."

Bisexual. He'd slipped it in so casually Shane almost hadn't noticed. He had no idea how he felt about that. He'd never given any thought to bisexuality. He'd heard all the usual assumptions of course but he'd somehow never believed it was an excuse for a sexual free-for-all. *Best not to react at all. Take it at face value. It's not as if it matters. Not for him and me anyway.*

"How about we get comfortable inside?" Chris nodded toward the hallway behind Shane. "Want another tinny?"

The sensible part of Shane's brain told him he should just go home. They'd had dinner together and it had been nice. If he left now they might be able to do it again someday as friends. Because he didn't have space in his life for anything beyond friendship. A far larger part of him was sick of being responsible. Surely he could look after number one every now and again. He liked Chris, enjoyed spending time with him and still couldn't get over the fact he'd stuck around despite Shane's less than flattering past.

"Sure, I'll have another cider."

He followed Chris into what was clearly the living room. The space and the furniture appeared comfortable and worn, as if it had been there for years and sprouted roots. He settled on the couch and wasn't surprised when Chris sat next to him.

"What about you?" Chris asked while studying his face. "America didn't agree with you?"

Bollix. For a moment Shane considered just telling Chris the whole sorry tale, before thinking better of it. They were having a nice, relaxing evening. Mentioning Ann and Danny now would not just bring the mood down but probably kill it altogether.

"Do you mind very much if we don't talk about that?" He stared at his hands. "I know it's not fair seeing how you just told me all about your mother, but I really wanted to get away from my own life for an evening." Shane glanced up at Chris' face just in time to see a frown disappear from

74

his forehead.

Chris nodded. "Fair enough." It was his turn to look away. "How long have you been in the tattoo business then?"

Shane was shocked to find his eyes burning as gratitude filled him. Maybe it was an Australian thing. Most Irish people wouldn't have dropped the subject so easily. Or maybe it was just that Chris was a good guy. *Too good for me.*

"I started as an apprentice when I was seventeen, so almost ten years now."

As they fell into an easy—and unthreatening—conversation about the job they both loved, Shane relaxed, the tension draining from his body. Chatting with Chris was as good as a massage. It was even better that Chris might as well be Irish when it came to talking. At some time during his ten years in Ireland he must have discovered the gift of the gab. Shane could limit himself to mostly listening, nodding at appropriate times and relaxing.

"Want another one?" Chris asked.

The question shook Shane out of his semi-sleep. He knew he should probably say no and go home but he was comfortable and for once not stressing about his life.

"One for the road."

He watched as Chris stood and walked away, then closed his eyes. *I'm not falling asleep. I'll just rest them for a moment.*

Chapter Ten

Chris stared into his fridge, his mind spinning with confused thoughts. He'd no idea what to make of Shane. The man went from open and engaging to closed off and almost angry in the blink of an eye. Try as he might, Chris had no way of telling whether or not Shane was interested in him. *Just my freaking luck.* For the first time in years Chris was experiencing a strong attraction to someone else and of course it had to be a man who probably didn't feel the same way.

He grabbed two cans, wondering what to do next. He'd run out of small talk. It was obvious Shane had no intention of talking about himself and Chris had shared all he wanted to say about his past.

He returned to the living room, struggling to come up with a topic—any topic—he could broach without turning the conversation heavy or personal, and came to a standstill.

A soft snoring sound greeted him. Shane's head had fallen back against the couch, his lips were slightly parted and he appeared relaxed to the point of being boneless— and fast asleep. Chris pushed down on the urge to brush his lips against Shane's, to push his tongue between them and wake him up with a sensual kiss, unsure how such a move would be welcomed…or not.

He lowered himself to the couch, taking care not to disturb Shane. If there was one thing Chris had no doubts about it was that everything about the man screamed exhaustion. Every time the two of them had met the dark shadows under Shane's eyes had been more pronounced, his cheeks more hollow and, now that Chris thought about it, his temper shorter. Should he just let him sleep? Maybe get something to cover him with and stretch him out across the couch? Or would it be better to wake him up and invite him to stay?

Taking advantage of the fact that he could do so unnoticed, Chris took his time to really study Shane's face. He looked so young and vulnerable. The sudden desire to protect Shane from whatever was bothering him took Chris by surprise. *For fuck sake, you barely know the man.*

The thought made up Chris' mind for him. He'd let Shane sleep for a while before waking him up. Whether he stayed here or went home was a decision he had to make for himself and if Chris had to take a guess he'd say Shane wouldn't appreciate it if Chris decided for him. He picked up the remote and turned on the TV, channel surfing until he found a mindless comedy quiz and settled back to watch it.

* * * *

An hour later, there was no sign of Shane being about to wake up. In fact, he hadn't moved at all since he'd dozed off, as far as Chris could tell. Maybe he should just get a blanket from upstairs, stretch Shane out on the couch and allow him to sleep through the night. Except that Chris knew from personal experience that a night on his couch led to days' worth of stiff muscles and aches. Shane wouldn't thank him if Chris allowed him to spend eight hours on this particular piece of furniture. Still, it was stupid how hard it was to reach out and gently shake Shane's shoulder when all his instincts told Chris the man needed this sleep.

Shane woke slowly, blinking and turning his head to take in his surroundings before focusing on Chris and straightening, a horrified expression on his face.

"Shit. I'm sorry. Did I fall asleep?"

Chris just nodded.

"Bollocks. Please tell me I wasn't out for long."

"About an hour." Chris said.

"That long? Why didn't you wake me up?"

Chris shrugged, suddenly uncomfortable and afraid he might have made the wrong decision after all. "You looked like you needed it."

Shane yawned in response, covering his mouth with his hand. "Thanks, I think." He pulled his phone from his pocket and checked the time. "I should go home. I'm crap company and we both need to work again tomorrow."

"Do you really need to go?" Chris leaned toward Shane, studying him intensely as he moved his mouth closer to his. Convinced that Shane would pull away and put distance between them, he had to remind himself to breathe as he slowly closed the distance between their lips. He saw the doubt in Shane's eyes, could almost hear his thoughts and had no problem imagining the argument the man might be having with himself.

When he brushed his lips across Shane's, Chris still wasn't sure how this move would be received, but a force stronger than his common sense pushed him forward. He couldn't explain the pull he felt toward Shane and, for the moment at least, he was disinclined to study it. He knew without a shadow of a doubt that if Shane pushed him away now he would have ruined any possibility of the two of them being friends, never mind anything more than that. Scaring Shane off was the last thing he wanted to do, but still Chris couldn't stop himself from pursuing the kiss and whatever might follow it.

Shane appeared frozen. He didn't try to get away but didn't make any move toward Chris either. When their mouths connected and Shane still didn't tell him to stop, Chris could breathe again. Shane's lips parted and Chris would have cheered if his mouth wasn't otherwise occupied. He put his hand at the back of Shane's neck and held him in a light grip, deepening the kiss at the same time. The soft sigh escaping Shane before he responded to the demands of Chris' mouth and tongue sounded like the sweetest music.

Chris lost himself in the kiss. The first time, two weeks earlier, they'd exchanged heat and need. This was something different—a getting to know each other, an exploration. Their tongues tangled with each other, alternating between demanding and caressing. Heat flowed through Chris' veins before heading south and filling his cock. *I want this man.* It wasn't about fucking him—Chris couldn't care less whether or not that would happen. He'd happily settle for sleeping with Shane in his bed, in his arms. He wanted to protect him from whatever horror was pursuing him and making him look exhausted enough to keel over.

When the need for a few steady breaths became too strong to ignore Chris pulled back. "Stay." It wasn't a question.

Shane stared into his eyes as if he was trying to find answers there.

"I'm not sure. I'm clearly crap company tonight." He averted his gaze. "I'm not up to anything. It's probably best if I go. I'm too tired…"

"All the more reason to stay. Why lose time you could spend sleeping on traveling back to where you live?"

Shane's eyes flashed with something Chris thought might well be suspicion. "Sleep. Right." The cynicism in Shane's voice shocked Chris until he remembered what Troy and Xander had told him. If Shane had only ever used men to get off with he was bound to distrust an offer of no-strings-attached sleep.

Chris pushed down the irritation bubbling up and smiled. "You are tired. I've got a comfortable bed. Let's sleep." He took Shane's hand without waiting for an answer and stood up, pulling Shane with him.

"I'd offer you my couch to sleep on but the thing will break your back. As for my spare room…" He cursed himself for never having gotten around to clearing the second bedroom out. "Well, the bed's unmade and hidden underneath years' worth of shit."

Several expressions flashed across Shane's face in quick succession, skepticism and resignation being the two Chris could easily identify. He told himself not to attach any meaning beyond exhaustion to the fact that Shane didn't protest and allowed himself to be led from the living room, through the hall and up the stairs to Chris' bedroom.

"You want to use the bathroom first?" Chris asked. "There's spare towels on the shelves and you'll find a new toothbrush in the cabinet underneath the sink. Help yourself."

Shane nodded, his face unreadable as he turned and walked toward the en suite. Chris kicked off his shoes and pulled his shirt over his head, tossing it into the hamper in the corner of his room. He had his hands on the button to undo his jeans before he thought better of it. If he was all but naked when Shane returned from the bathroom he would never believe Chris had meant it when he said they would sleep. He lowered himself to the side of the bed and waited, wondering again why he was feeling so protective of Shane. He'd never before felt the need to come to someone's rescue the way he did now and he had no idea what to make of the impulse. The fact that he'd no way of knowing whether Shane needed rescuing and if so from what, only made his actions all the more bewildering.

When Shane returned to the bedroom he paused for a moment. Heat flared in his eyes as he took in Chris' naked torso before he averted his gaze again. Reluctant to break the barely comfortable silence, Chris got up and brushed past Shane to take care of his own nighttime ablutions. Five minutes later, when he returned, Shane was in his bed, the thin duvet pulled up to his chin, leaving only his face visible, his eyes open but heavy with sleep.

"Comfortable?"

Chris turned off the light before taking off his jeans and joining Shane.

"Yes. You weren't joking when you said you had a comfortable bed. I could happily spend my life here."

Wouldn't mind if you did.

Fuck. Where did that thought come from?

"Memory foam will do that for you," he said, determined to keep the moment casual.

"Hmmmm, I may have to get one of those for myself." Shane sounded barely awake so Chris didn't reply. A few moments later soft snores filled the room again.

It had been too long since he'd shared his bed with someone else. It should have been strange, not having the full width of it to himself, but felt just right instead. It would be even better if he could wrap his arms around Shane, pull him close and sleep entwined. He turned onto his side and studied the shadowy outline of Shane on the pillow next to his. He was so close. He wouldn't have to reach far to touch him. He resisted the urge, convinced that Shane wouldn't welcome being grabbed just after he'd fallen asleep.

Chris closed his eyes and allowed the sound of soft snores to lull him to sleep too. His last thought before he dozed off was that this had probably been the most bizarre date night he'd ever experienced.

* * * *

"Where are you going?"

Chris kept his voice soft and his tone mild. He'd woken to find himself alone in bed with Shane standing near the door, pulling on his trousers. The room was dark, only the glow of street lights filtering through the curtains, which meant it had to be the middle of the night.

Everything Chris knew about Shane told him the man spooked easily and that was the last thing he wanted to do. Not until he was sure he had a reason to be upset anyway. He reached out and turned on his bedside light.

"Home." Shane looked anywhere except at Chris' face.

"Without waking me up and saying goodbye?" Chris asked, again making sure his voice held no accusatory note, just curiosity.

Even in the faint light from his bedside lamp Chris recognized the heat rushing to Shane's cheeks. "Maybe I am that big a bastard after all."

A smile tugged at Chris' lips as he slowly shook his head. "I don't think so. Whatever is going on with you right now, I don't think it has anything to do with you being a bastard." *Please let me be right about that.*

Shane opened his mouth to interrupt, but Chris continued before he had a chance.

"I know you're not going to tell me what *is* going on, and that's fine. But don't be a fool. Stay. Come back to bed and sleep. The fact that you do doesn't have to mean anything unless you want it to."

"I don't get it." Shane didn't push his trousers down but, much to Chris' relief, he made no move to put his shirt on either. "Why are you doing this? What are you getting out of it?"

Now we're getting to the crux of the matter. "Who says I need to get anything out of you sleeping in my bed?" Chris asked. "You look and sound exhausted. Why does my invitation have to be anything other than an offer to help?"

Shane sat down at the bottom of the bed, his face turned away from Chris. "Because it doesn't work like that. Not in my life. There's always a price."

Chris cursed the fact that he couldn't see Shane's expressions. His tone of voice held a distinct note of despair, but without being able to see his face Chris couldn't be sure he'd heard him right.

"This isn't just about your life though, is it?" He asked, picking his words carefully despite his sleep-addled brain making it hard to think straight. "I don't keep tabs. You don't owe me anything just because I fed you and allowed you to sleep here." His irritation got the better of him. "Don't confuse me with someone I'm not."

Shane laughed, although the sound was anything but happy. "Don't project my habits on you. Isn't that what you mean?" He turned around and despite the insufficient light in his bedroom Chris thought he could make out the distress on Shane's face.

Chris sighed. "No! Maybe." He thought for a moment. "Fuck it, no, that's not what I meant. I just don't want you judging me on the basis of other people's habits." He took a deep breath, forcing himself to stay calm. "It's the middle of the night. Take your trousers off again and go back to sleep. If you really want to have this discussion we can talk in the morning."

Shane muttered something under his breath and got up. For a few moments, Chris had no idea what Shane might do next and he figured the man standing two meters away didn't know either. Then Shane pushed his trousers down, walked around the bed and snuggled back under the covers, all of it without once looking at Chris.

He reached out and tugged at Shane's shoulder until he turned and faced him. "Stop overthinking this. We're sleeping. I like you. If you let me I'd like to get to know you better, but it doesn't have to happen now." He smiled, the need to take care of Shane getting the upper hand again. "Close your eyes and go back to sleep."

Chris reached behind him, blindly searching for the light switch with his hand.

"Wait a moment," Shane said as he scrutinized Chris' face. "I don't get you. But I think… I hope I can trust you." He blinked a few times, as if his eyelids were getting too heavy again, and yawned.

Unable to resist, Chris stroked a finger across Shane's face, tracing his lips, cheeks and eyes. When Shane didn't turn away Chris cupped the back of his neck and pulled him closer until Shane's face rested on his shoulder. Shane stiffened against him before relaxing.

"That's it. Now sleep."

Minutes later Shane drifted off while Chris held him, unable to find the peace of mind necessary to follow him into sleep. He'd absolutely no idea what he was doing but he couldn't escape the feeling that he might be setting himself up for a world filled with pain. If only he could be sure he could trust the quiet voice in the back of his mind telling him it would all be worth it in the long run.

Chapter Eleven

"And then we built a huge sandcastle. And I had three buckets and…"

Shane allowed Danny's excited voice to wash over him as the boy told his mother all about the three days he'd spent by the seaside. He could see Ann was struggling and didn't know how much longer he'd be able to allow the lad to ramble on, but for the moment both mother and son appeared to need this connection.

The few short days in different surroundings had clearly done Danny the world of good. *Ma looks less tired too.* Shane studied his mother, who looked at her daughter and grandson with an obviously fake smile plastered on her face.

As for Shane, he felt less exhausted than he had for the past few months too. A lot of that was a result of the uninterrupted nights he'd been able to enjoy without Danny's regular nightmares waking him up.

And Chris.

Much as Shane didn't want to admit it, his evening and night with Chris had done a lot to lower his stress levels.

"And guess what, Mammy?"

Danny's words broke through his thoughts.

Ann, in a tired voice, replied, "You saw a dinosaur."

Shane smiled.

"No!" Danny giggled. "Silly Mammy. There are no dinosaurs at the beach. I got an ice cream every day."

The voice slipped into the background again. Shane had already listened to Danny's beach adventures twice and knew the story off by heart.

He still couldn't get his head around the night he'd spent in Chris' bed. The man hadn't made a move on him, much to Shane's surprise. Even when Shane had reached for Chris' cock when they woke up on Friday morning – thinking that an orgasm was the least he could do in return for the night of restful sleep – Chris had pushed his hand away.

'Don't. There's no need for that. I didn't ask you to stay so I could get off.' The words still didn't make sense to Shane. What other reason could he have to invite a man into his house, his bed? Not understanding didn't stop him from appreciating what Chris had done though. He'd felt good that night and was grateful he hadn't managed to sneak out when he'd tried to do so. It would have been a despicable stunt to pull.

He studied his sister's face and recognized the exhaustion, the effort she made to hide the worst of the pain she felt from her young son. She always asked the medical staff to give her fewer painkillers when Danny came to visit, wanting to be more or less lucid for the short time she got to spend with him, but it cost her. He'd give it a few more minutes before separating mother and son again.

Shane's thoughts returned to what had become a favorite escape from the horrid reality of his life again. *Chris.* Under any other circumstances he might have been tempted to experiment. Never before had he thought of a man as more than an opportunity for sex. Fast, furious, orgasmic and a one-off were the only expectations he'd ever had. Chris had aroused other feelings in him. He wanted to get to know him, find out what made Chris tick and try to figure out why he seemed to approach life in what Shane saw as a strange manner. Just his luck he'd run into him now. Between his job, Ann's illness and taking care of Danny the last thing Shane needed was yet another commitment to slot into his life. Timing was everything and right now it was completely wrong.

Ann's exhaustion became more apparent and Shane knew she wouldn't last much longer. He really couldn't wait much longer before giving her a break from her much-loved but exhausting son.

The conversation he'd had with Chris when he left after their night together replayed in his mind.

'Give me your number.' Chris said.

Shane actually extracted his phone from his pocket and pulled up the contacts screen before pushing it into his pocket again. What was the point? He could exchange numbers but all it would lead to was him having to tell Chris he didn't have time to meet up. Much better to put an end to any and all expectations now. So he told Chris he only used the phone for emergencies and that he could always be reached at work. The expression on Chris' face after he'd finished talking made Shane feel like a dick. Still, it had to be better to disappoint him in one harsh moment than over several long weeks while he either refused to accept calls or rejected invitations to meet up. Life's a bitch and then... He didn't finish the thought – it cut too close to home.

The pitch in Danny's voice got higher and Shane recognized the boy was close to reaching his limits too.

"Ma, why don't you take Danny to the cafeteria for a treat?" He kept his voice casual while trying to urge her on with his eyes. Surely she also recognized that Danny was on the verge of breaking down. Ann didn't need to see that.

She nodded and turned to Danny. "What would you like, pet?"

"Can I have a Coke and one of those chocolate cakes?" Danny smiled up at his granny as he pressed his luck on the back of that generous and open offer.

"I think we can do that."

Ann held it together until her son and mother had left the room. As soon as the door closed behind them the first tears rolled down her cheeks. "It's so hard." She whispered the words, her voice choked.

Shane got up and carefully sat on the edge of his sister's bed, opening his arms as he did so. "Come here. You don't have to be brave all the time."

"I want him to remember me as happy, not as a crying

wreck."

Tears burned behind Shane's eyes as his sister rested her head on his shoulder and allowed herself a very rare crying spell despite the pain the movement and contact had to cause her.

"I'll make sure he always knows how wonderful and special you are. He'll never doubt you loved him, that he was the most important thing in your life." Speaking got harder with every word he said. The unfairness of the whole situation washed over him once again. Danny deserved to have his mother around as he grew up. Ann should be there for Danny's first day in school and for every other big event in his life. He fought the urge but couldn't stop one tear escaping from his eye.

Ann slowly pulled back until she rested against her pillows again and looked at Shane, a sad smile tugging at her lips when she noticed how close to the surface his emotions were. "You don't have to be strong all the time either, you know. It's okay to be scared and angry."

Maybe it is. Maybe he could be honest about his feelings, just for once. "How am I going to do it, sis? I'm not good enough to raise him. He deserves so much better."

"Don't be silly." Ann's voice was gentle, her expression soft. "Of course you're good enough. You're just having to grow up faster than you were planning on. I wouldn't trust anybody else with my little boy. I *know* you won't let us down."

Shane knew no such thing but he did know he'd die trying. He'd be the best man he could possibly be. If only he could have more time to get used to the situation, to wrap his head around the idea of being the guardian of a young boy, to figure out what it would mean and how he would manage it.

"Shane?" Ann's voice was so soft he had to strain to hear her.

"Yes, princess."

"I don't think I have much longer. I don't know...I just

can't do this anymore. It hurts too much. I need it to stop."

Panic squeezed his stomach. He'd known this moment would come when he got on a plane to fly home from Florida. There'd never been any hope that somehow a miracle would happen and still it was too soon. He wouldn't wish the suffering his sister had been going through on his worst enemy and yet he selfishly wished she'd hang on for another few weeks...months. Platitudes burned on his lips. He yearned to tell her that she was just extra tired because Danny had visited, that she would feel better as soon as she'd rested, but he knew those words would be lies.

"I know." He swallowed hard, knowing he needed to be stronger than he felt. "It's okay if you need to let go. Don't worry about us, we'll manage. I don't know how exactly but we will."

She forced another smile. "I know you will. And I'm sorry for giving up. I never thought there'd come a moment when I wanted to die, but I do. This..." She pointed at herself. "This isn't living."

"You're not afraid to die?"

"No, I'm not. I used to be, but no longer." She closed her eyes and Shane could see her gathering whatever reserves of strength she might have had left. "I hate that I won't be around to see Danny grow up. I'm so sorry Ma will have to bury me. No parent should have to go through that. And I never meant to mess up your life."

Shane opened his mouth to tell her she was doing no such thing but a gentle shake of Ann's head shut him up before he could start.

"I've been thinking about this and I think dying is worse for those who stay behind than it is for the one leaving. Whatever does or doesn't come after I die, it will be different from life as I know it. It's you and Ma and Danny who'll have to keep on living the same life but now with a huge Ann or Mammy or daughter-shaped hole in it."

Fuck! Shane's tentative grasp on his emotions slipped and tears spilled from his eyes before he realized what was happening. He could feel the Ann-shaped hole in his heart. It had started as a small tear created the moment he'd first seen her in hospital and it had grown from there. He'd never thought about it in those terms, but they fit how he felt perfectly.

Shit. Shit. Shit. He didn't want to cry. Ann had more than enough to deal with without him adding his pain and despair to her burden but for once his resolve failed him.

"It's okay, Shane, cry. You don't always have to be the tough one." Ann's voice was gentle. "You've always hidden your emotions. I can't remember the last time I saw you in tears."

Only because you're not with me in the middle of the night when Danny wakes up from yet another nightmare and I can't figure out how to keep going or how to make things better.

Helpless to stop them, Shane allowed the tears to fall. Maybe it was for the best if he got it out of the way now. He would need to be strong for his mother and Danny when Ann did die, and he knew that could be any day now. If he shed the tears now he might be able to contain them then. His phone vibrated in his pocket and he wiped his cheeks before retrieving it.

Coming up again.

Gratitude that his mother had had the insight to give him a heads-up filled Shane. "They're on their way back."

Ann nodded but didn't open her eyes.

"I'll let Danny say goodbye to you and then we'll take him home. I think it's been more than enough for both of you."

"Thank you." Ann opened her eyes and for a moment Shane could see his sister as she used to be. "I love you, Shane. You're a good man. Don't let anybody tell you otherwise." She swallowed hard. "If there is such a thing as an afterlife I'll never be far away, believe me."

No! Not yet. I'm not ready.

He knew she was saying goodbye, that she'd given up the fight and was ready to go. He hated himself for being selfish enough to wish that she'd hang on for longer but he couldn't stop the self-serving thought.

"Mammy?"

Shane had been so caught up in his own pain he hadn't heard the door open and Danny's plaintive voice took him by surprise.

"Hey, baby." Ann sounded exhausted and Shane marveled that she managed to drag up the strength to open her eyes again and smile at her son. "Mammy's tired now and needs to sleep. You go home with Nanny and Uncle Shane. Remember to be a good boy, okay?"

"Yes, Mammy." Danny approached the bed cautiously, as if he could sense the danger lurking there.

Knowing what was expected of him, Shane lifted Danny up so he could kiss his mother's cheek without Ann having to move. "Love you, Mammy."

"Love you more, munchkin." Ann gave the standard response with hardly any trace of strain in her voice.

Shane lowered Danny to the floor and bent to kiss his sister.

"Love you, princess. Don't worry about us. We'll manage. I'll find a way." He could only hope he'd whispered the words softly enough for Danny not to have heard them.

"Danny and I will wait for you outside, Ma." He held out his hand and turned to the door as soon as Danny took it, making sure not to look at his mother for fear of losing it again.

* * * *

He allowed Danny to run around the garden in front of the hospice while they waited for his mother to join them. When she walked out the front door fifteen minutes later it was clear she'd been crying too. Shane wanted to gather her in a hug but stopped himself, afraid that such a gesture would only alert Danny to his granny's distress.

"Why don't we go into town and get Danny his school uniform?" he suggested. Anything would be better than going home right now. The idea of being surrounded by the life Ann had created for herself and the boy suddenly felt too hard to bear and it was only another two weeks before the boy would start in junior infants.

Shane watched his mother as she glanced at Danny and visibly gathered herself. He was able to hear her thoughts as if she'd said the words out loud because the same sentiment ran through his mind. *We shouldn't be doing this. Ann should be taking him shopping.*

"Yes, let's do that. And maybe we'll make a day of it." She winked at Danny. "Buying your first uniform is a big deal. I think that deserves a dinner in McDonald's, what do you think?"

A huge grin appeared on the boy's face. He probably couldn't believe his luck at being allowed Coke, cake and a Happy Meal all in one afternoon. Not for the first time since he'd returned to Ireland, Shane wished he was Danny's age and as easily distracted from the pain in his life. Being a grownup and especially having to act like one sucked.

Chapter Twelve

Chris turned the corner and looked up at the now familiar shop sign just a bit farther down the street. This would be his third week working at VikInk and he wasn't sure what to expect.

He'd thought the evening and night he and Shane had spent together might have made them closer but the next morning Shane had still refused to exchange phone numbers.

'I'd rather not.' Shane avoided his gaze. *'I only really use it for emergencies. If you need me you can reach me in work.'*

Chris wasn't going to lie to himself. The refusal had hurt. He also couldn't deny that he had been tempted to call VikInk's number. Not a day had gone by when he hadn't scrolled through the names in his phone only to not press the call button.

Mixed signals didn't begin to describe the vibes he got from Shane. He wanted to believe the man felt at least some of the attraction Chris experienced every time he was close to Shane, but whenever he figured that yes, it was a mutual thing, Shane would do something to destroy the illusion.

He cursed under his breath. He was thirty-five years old, for fuck sake — this whole situation was ridiculous. He was long past playing 'will he, won't he' games. Today he'd sort the whole mess out. He'd just ask the question while they were having lunch together. Either Shane was interested or not. It was time to find out what the answer was. As much as he didn't want to consider the possibility, Chris had to accept that it was conceivable that Shane was exactly as big a dick as Troy and Xander had told him he was. His instincts told him something else was going on, but he wasn't sure he could trust his intuition when it came to Shane. Maybe he saw what he wanted to see and not what was actually there.

When he was two doors away from his destination, his phone buzzed in his pocket. Walking on, he retrieved it, frowning when he saw Troy's name on the display. *What does he want? He knows I'm not coming into Pins & Needles today.*

He pressed the answer button the same moment he came to a halt in front of VikInk. The parlor was closed, all the lights were off and a note had been stuck to the window.

Closed due to bereavement. We apologize for any inconvenience and will re-open tomorrow.

He heard Troy's voice in his ear without understanding the words.

"Sorry, could you repeat all of that?"

"I'm sorry," Troy said. "I should have called you earlier. You're probably almost at VikInk by now."

"Standing in front of it, actually. Except that it's closed."

"Yeah, that's why I'm calling. There's no need for you to go in today."

"Obviously." Chris wasn't sure whether he was more frustrated about the wasted journey or the idea that he wouldn't see Shane and therefore wouldn't be able to get the answers he so desperately needed. "Who died?"

"Shane's sister," Troy answered. "I didn't even know she was unwell, but apparently she's been sick for quite some time. Barry didn't give me any details, but the impression I got is that it's all quite horrible."

"Shit." Suddenly Shane's reluctance to get involved with Chris and his refusal to share his phone number made a lot of sense.

"Do you know where the funeral is taking place?" He paused for a moment. "I mean, you don't need me to come into Pins & Needles today, do you?"

"No, I don't need you here. I've not taken any Thursday bookings for you. You want to go to the funeral?"

It was a very good question. Chris had never gotten used to the Irish habit of just showing up at funerals no matter how tenuous the connection to the deceased might be, and he didn't know Shane's sister at all. In fact, he hadn't even known Shane had a sister, never mind that she'd been ill. On the other hand, he had grown close to Shane and wanted to support him.

"Yeah, I do." He thought about the fraught relationship between Shane and Troy and continued. "That's not a problem, is it?"

"No, of course not," Troy said. "Fuck, I've even thought about going myself. I met his sister once or twice. She was a lovely girl." He fell silent for a moment. "I decided against it because I don't think a funeral is the best place for me and Shane to come face to face for the first time after all that happened."

"So, where do I go?" Chris asked.

"Right. The mass is in the Church of Saint Agatha on William Street North at eleven. You know where that is?"

"I'll find it."

"When you talk to him, would you tell him...? No, actually say nothing. He really doesn't need to be reminded of me today. I'll see you tomorrow."

"See you then, boss." Chris ended the call and stared at the dark interior of VikInk for a few more moments before turning on his heel and heading back the way he'd come. He'd go home and change. If he was going to a funeral the least he could do was show a proper amount of respect.

* * * *

Almost two hours after his conversation with Troy, Chris came to a standstill and stared at the church. The gray bricks almost made the place look unassuming, except that the size of the building made it stand out in the street. People were entering in small groups, their voices too soft for Chris to hear their words.

Not for the first time he wondered whether attending the funeral was the right thing to do. Knowing that the Irish traditionally took paying their respects to what he considered to be extreme lengths didn't mean he'd ever gotten used to it. It had been especially hard when he'd had to bury his grandmother. The endless stream of people he'd never met before, all coming to shake his hand and commiserating with him, had been disturbing. He'd loved knowing that his granny was remembered fondly by so many, but he'd had no idea what he was supposed to say to or do with all those strangers he'd never met before and would probably never see again.

He pushed his doubts away. Shane was Irish. Chris would have to trust that meant he was used to Irish customs and would appreciate the support. Taking a deep breath, he forced himself to cross the last few meters between himself and the church entrance.

The inside of the church was much brighter than Chris had expected. White walls and plenty of windows gave the place an almost cheerful vibe. He imagined that would be wonderful for couples getting married, or baptisms, but it felt almost inappropriate for a funeral.

Glancing around, he spotted Barry and others he recognized from VikInk. He considered joining them until he realized how squashed together they already were in their pew and settled for a seat on the back row.

Soft conversations took place all around him and it was impossible not to hear parts of them. He learned that Shane's sister had been sick for months. Someone expressed their admiration for Shane, who'd apparently abandoned a promising career in America to come home as soon as she'd been diagnosed. More than one person commented on the poor little orphan, and Chris couldn't help wondering who that might be.

Only a few minutes later the mass started. Chris was shocked to discover how hard it was to listen to the words he'd last heard when he buried his grandmother. That had been five years ago and he'd thought he'd long since come to terms with that loss, but suddenly the pain was back with a vengeance, reminding him of the permanency of death.

As the mass progressed to the presentation of the gifts, Chris noticed the small boy for the first time. He slowly approached the altar, holding Shane's hand while clutching a picture frame to his chest. The tear-streaked cheeks combined with the determined expression on his little face tore at Chris' heart. He remembered how devastated he'd been when his mother had told him she was done mothering on his eighteenth birthday and tried to imagine what it might be like losing a parent at this lad's young age. His imagination wasn't up to the task.

He kept his eyes on Shane, who appeared exhausted, and the little boy until they sat down in their pew, then forced himself to look away. It was no good. Every few seconds his gaze would find Shane again and a deep-rooted need to take him in his arms and hold him close, to create a barrier between him and his obvious pain, filled Chris.

He zoned out of the mass, going through the motions of standing up, sitting down, kneeling and exchanging the sign of peace on automatic pilot. It wasn't until a middle-aged lady stood and proceeded to the altar to give a eulogy that Chris snapped out of his self-indulgent distraction to give her words his full attention.

Everything about the woman shouted her devastation — the way she moved, the gray tone of her skin and her almost stooped stance behind the lectern. But when she opened her mouth her voice was strong, with only the occasional wobble betraying her despair, while her words spoke of love, fond memories and hope for the future despite the present pain. Her speech was short, heart-wrenching and touching.

She returned to her seat and Chris watched as she

reached for the small boy sitting on Shane's lap. A loud wail reverberated through the church as the child clutched at Shane, unwilling to release his hold despite both the woman and Shane talking to him. After a few moments of this Shane shrugged and turned toward the altar with the boy still in his arms.

"My sister was a remarkable woman." Shane sounded on the verge of tears. "Of course, as her only brother I have to say that, but everybody who has ever met her will know those words are true. She had so much love to give and gave it so freely. She didn't know how to be selfish and always put others ahead of herself. She would be the first to tell you that the best thing she ever did was to give birth to this amazing boy. Just as she told me that the hardest part of dying was having to leave Danny behind." A choked sob interrupted Shane's flow of words and for a moment he stared at the people in front of him.

Chris couldn't keep his eyes off Shane. The man standing there, holding the boy close, took his breath away. When Shane's gaze came to rest on him, Chris nodded slowly. *I'm here for you.* He wished he could shout he words.

"It's no false modesty when I say that I'm not good enough to stand in my sister's shadow, but I will do what I can to be who she expected me to be. She's entrusted me with the care of Danny and I'm determined he will never want for anything and will always know how loved he is, how special his mother was and how much she adored him. Thank you for coming. Ann would have loved to see you all. She would also have told us to stop being so gloomy and to concentrate on the good memories rather than the sad parting. I therefore invite all of you to join us in Cusack's for soup, sandwiches and stories about the amazing girl I was lucky enough to have for my big sister for twenty-seven years."

Tears burned in Chris' eyes for a woman he had never known, her young orphaned son and a man he'd only met a few weeks before. Blinking furiously, he watched as

Shane stepped away from the lectern and joined his mother again. Chris barely heard the priest as he went through the concluding rites, lost in thought as to how he might be able to help Shane, wondering whether or not he would accept assistance and trying to figure out how to phrase the offer.

With almost everybody else in the church Chris waited as Shane, the young boy still in his arms and the woman who had to be his mother walked to the side of the altar and took up position there. A young woman stepped up to a microphone and sang the first words of *In the Arms of an Angel* as a line formed and people took turns offering their condolences. Chris remained seated, trying to figure out whether or not he should go up and offer his. What could he possibly say beyond 'I'm so sorry for your loss', words Shane would have heard countless times before Chris even reached him? Would it make a difference to Shane whether he did or not?

He thought back to his grandmother's funeral and tried to remember how he'd felt when stranger after stranger had come up to him to shake his hand and talk to him for a few short moments. It had been strange, but after he'd gotten over his initial surprise, not uncomfortable. Quite the opposite in fact. He'd taken great solace from the fact his granny had been loved. And Chris wanted Shane to know he would be there for him, should he want the support. Besides, although he'd only met Shane a few weeks ago they most definitely weren't strangers. It really wasn't a question. Of course he would join the queue.

As he stood and took his place at the end of the line of people still waiting he realized the problem wasn't whether or not he needed to say something to Shane but if he would be able to stop himself from pulling him into his arms.

The line made slow but steady progress and it wasn't long until Chris found himself face to face with Shane. He stared into his unblinking, honey-colored eyes. His face appeared to be sculpted out of granite, without a trace of any emotions he might be experiencing.

"I'm so sorry for your loss," Chris said. "If there's anything I can do…" The words felt so empty and inadequate.

Shane's mask slipped for a moment and he squeezed his eyes shut. When he opened them again, his gaze was once again closed-off and hard.

"Thank you for coming. It means a lot." Shane's voice was barely audible.

Lost for words Chris nodded, gripped Shane's shoulder and squeezed softly, hoping the gesture would express all the things he couldn't put into words, before moving on to Shane's mother.

"You don't know me, Mrs. Boyle. My name is Chris and I wanted to let you know how sorry I am for your loss. No parent should have to go through something like this."

"Thank you. You're a friend of my son's?"

"I…" *What the fuck am I?* "I hope so."

"Good." Her lips stretched into a small smile. "He needs all the friends he can get. You'll be joining us in the pub, right."

It wasn't a question and despite his decision not to go there, Chris suddenly found he couldn't come up with a good reason to refuse her. He glanced back and found Shane staring at him. As hard as it was to read Shane's expression, Chris thought he saw hope there and suddenly it wasn't a difficult question anymore.

"I'll be there. Thank you for inviting me." He stepped back and watched as the priest joined Shane and his family. He wouldn't go to the cemetery but he could wait for them in Cusack's.

Outside the church people waited in small groups, talking more freely now and he even heard laughter.

"Chris!"

He looked around until he saw Barry gesturing at him and redirected his steps to where the VikInk crew had gathered.

"Did Troy get to you on time?" Barry asked as soon as Chris reached him. "I completely forgot you were supposed to work with us today. And I don't have your number on my mobile, only on the shop phone."

"Don't worry about it." Chris shrugged. "My wasted journey is rather insignificant given the rest of the day, don't you think?"

"Yeah. I guess. Thank you for taking it so well. Are you staying on?"

"I was thinking of going to the pub now," Chris replied. "I'll wait for the rest of them there."

"So are we," Barry said. "You might as well join us."

Chris nodded. He'd feel a little bit less like a fish out of water if he knew at least a few people in the crowd of strangers he'd otherwise find himself in.

"Thanks. I will."

Silence descended again as the coffin was pushed out of the church, followed by Shane and his mother, the young boy now walking between them and holding hands with both his granny and his uncle.

I'll find a way to help you. Chris made the silent vow as he followed Shane with his eyes. He'd figure out how to make himself useful and it had nothing to do with wanting Shane in his arms and his bed again.

Chapter Thirteen

"I have to say it came as a huge shock when he called and told me he needed to take time off because his sister had died. I had no idea there was anything wrong with the woman." Barry picked up his pint and took a sip before putting it down again. "I had a feeling something had to be going on when he suddenly returned from America after literally burning all his ships behind him when he left, but he never told me his reasons for returning when he asked for his old job back." Barry stared off into the distance for a moment before continuing. "And I stopped asking after not getting an answer the first time I did. I wish I hadn't. I'm sure I could have done more if I'd known. I mean, working full time on top of dealing with the turmoil in his private life must have been killing him. No wonder he constantly looked exhausted."

As Chris listened to Barry he couldn't help feeling guilty too. He'd noticed how tired Shane looked and he'd wondered about his reluctance to stay in touch. If he'd paid more attention he might have realized it wasn't Shane being coy but a real issue. He'd been so sure he hadn't allowed Troy and Xander's stories to cloud his judgement but maybe he *had* been expecting the worst from Shane rather than giving him the benefit of the doubt. *There's no fucking maybe about it.*

Still, there was very little he could do about the past. He could, however, try to help now that he did know what had been going on. If Shane would let him. If he'd been too proud to tell people about the issues he was dealing with before today, there was a good chance he'd be no more willing to accept assistance now.

"So where does this leave you?" Chris asked Barry. "You were understaffed before this happened. It must be even worse now." He needed to get his mind off Shane for a while. He wouldn't be able to work out where to go from here until he'd had an opportunity to talk to the man and today was probably not the day for that conversation to take place.

Barry snorted. "In trouble?" He drank some more from his pint. "I told Shane to take as much time as he needs before coming back to work. I guess the rest of us will just have to work longer hours until he returns." He shrugged. "It is what it is. I'll figure it out. Many of the clients booked in with Shane asked for him specifically and I expect they'd rather wait for his return than switch to someone else. It might not be as bad as it could be."

Chris glanced at his watch, wondering how long it would be until the funeral party would return from the cemetery when the door to the pub opened and a large group of people entered. He automatically searched out Shane and his heart squeezed in his chest when he found him.

Chris remembered the somewhat cocky man he'd first met in the pub, how stand-offish and defensive Shane had been when they'd met again and compared the memory to what he saw now. He'd never seen this version of Shane before and wouldn't have been able to imagine this incarnation of him. This man, wearing a dark suit and carrying a young boy in his arms, appeared to have nothing in common with the smart-arsed bordering on arrogant person he'd first met and — he could be honest about it now — had started to fall for. It was hard to believe this was the Shane who had selfishly waltzed all over Troy and Xander. All Chris saw was a broken being, someone holding on to his sanity with an almost desperate grip. All his instincts told Chris to approach him, to tell him he'd do whatever he could to help Shane but he stayed where he was, picked up his pint and drained it.

Shane was surrounded by those closest to him and Chris had no doubt he'd be intruding where he wasn't wanted if he joined the group. He didn't know Shane well enough, didn't know the rest of his family at all. Maybe he should just leave. This wasn't getting anybody anywhere. Shane had far more important things to deal with right now than the feelings Chris was developing for him. He made up his mind to leave when somebody placed another pint in front of him.

Time passed slowly as people talked and drank. Bar staff entered the lounge with platters filled with sandwiches and trays holding soup bowls. Chris noticed the young boy wriggling in Shane's arms before being lowered to the ground and taking off at a run.

"Danny!" Both Shane and his mother shouted the name at the same time as the boy raced across the pub toward where Chris and the rest of VikInk's staff were sitting, on a clear collision course with a lounge girl serving soup. On instinct, Chris reached out, scooped the boy up and pulled him onto his lap before he'd run into the waitress and ended up covered in the hot substance.

"Hey there, little bugger, if you go any faster you'll take off."

The boy stared at him from a tear-stained face.

"You are fast. You don't play football by any chance, do you?"

The boy visibly relaxed and Chris wondered if people at this funeral talked to him the way they'd spoken to Chris at his granny's funeral. If he had had a hard time dealing with the constant questions about how he was and the endless stream of well-meaning but devastating sympathy, he could only imagine what it had to be like for one so young who could probably barely make sense of what had just happened to his life anyway.

"Not yet. But I'll be starting soon." A very small smile appeared on Danny's face.

"Really? Which club?" Chris asked.

"Orchard United of course." The boy looked at him as if he couldn't believe an adult could be so silly.

"Cool," Chris said. "Wanna know a secret?" He bent closer to the boy and semi-whispered the question.

Danny nodded, apparently enthralled.

"I know who your trainer is going to be."

"Oh." Danny stared at him with huge eyes. "Is he nice? I'm not very good yet."

"I think so." Chris smiled. "His name is Chris."

The boy studied him. "Isn't that your name?" Clearly he'd been paying attention to the conversations going on around him in church, if he remembered that.

"You know what? I think you're right."

The boy giggled, momentarily forgetting all about the turmoil in his life as only children were able to do.

"Hey, munchkin." Shane's voice came from behind Chris. "I hope you're not bothering the guests."

"He's fine." Chris hastened to reassure Shane. "We've been talking about football, haven't we?" He glanced at Danny who nodded enthusiastically. "Turns out I'm going to be his football trainer when he starts at Orchard United."

"Really?" Shane's solemn mask slipped for a moment to be replaced by first surprise then something looking a lot like suspicion.

Chris ignored the implied accusation. "I've been training the junior team there for two years now. I love it. The kids are great and it gets me out and about."

Shane studied Chris as if trying to determine the truth of his words before nodding.

"What do you think of that, lad?" he asked Danny. "You already know your trainer. How cool is that?"

The boy grinned at Shane whose expression relaxed too. The obvious love between boy and man took Chris' breath away and for a moment he wished Troy and Xander could see this version of Shane. No matter how much of a dickhead he'd been in the past, Shane had clearly got his priorities sorted now.

Chris turned to his side, noticed Barry was no longer sitting next to him and moved over with Danny still in his lap.

"Sit down for a moment," he said, staring up at Shane. "No offense, but you look about ready to collapse."

Shane all but fell onto the seat. "That sounds about right," he muttered. "Thanks for intercepting the boy. For a moment I was certain he was going to end up covered in soup. I don't know what got into him but I probably shouldn't have allowed him to get away from me."

"Don't mention it," Chris said. "I get it. If these situations are hard on adults, it must be even worse for kids. They pick up on the stress but have no frame of reference for what's going on around them. It's only natural he's playing up." He stopped talking before he said too much.

"And it's bound to get worse before it gets better," Shane said, apparently understanding exactly what Chris meant. "There are times I'm jealous of his ability to live in the moment and to just forget the drama his life has turned into for a while." He inhaled sharply and blinked, apparently shocked by what he'd just said. "Anyway, I'd better join me ma again. Thanks again for catching Danny when you did." Shane turned to Danny. "Come along, lad." He held out his hand.

"No!" The happy boy who'd been smiling a moment ago disappeared in an instant. "I want to stay with him." Danny pointed at Chris. "You're no fun."

Shane blanched as if he had been slapped. "Not now, Danny. I need you to behave." The pleading note in Shane's voice was painful to hear.

"It's okay. Leave him with me." Chris caught the attention of a waitress collecting empty platters from the tables. "You wouldn't have a deck of cards, would you?" he asked.

"Sure, give me a minute." The girl smiled, scurried off and returned a few moments later with a box of playing cards in her hand. "There you go."

"You know how to play snap?" Chris asked Danny.

"Yes!" The boy smiled again. "And I always win."

"But you haven't played against me yet." Chris grinned at Danny and was delighted to see the determined expression on the young boy's face. Shane had been right—it was easy to distract the lad.

"Go on. Do what you have to do. Stay with your mother. Danny's fine with me. If he gets too much for me I'll let you know, but don't hold your breath. After all, I train about twenty of these little monkeys for two hours most Wednesday evenings."

Shane's expression changed from relieved to worried and back again. "If you're sure?"

"I am." Chris lowered his voice. "Let me help. It's little enough. You don't have to do it all on your own, you know."

Shane opened his mouth as if to reply before closing it again, nodding and getting up. "Thanks." He turned his gaze to Danny. "You be good."

The boy had taken the cards from the package and was trying to shuffle them, dropping several of them to the floor. "Yes, Uncle Shane," he said as he jumped off Chris' lap to pick the cards up again.

Chris fully expected to have to the let the boy win but the little bugger was a shark with hands as fast as the speed of light. Even when Chris took the game seriously and tried to slap his hand on top of the pile of cards when two matching images showed up, the lad beat him more often than not.

"I guess nobody warned you he's an expert at this game." The soft, gentle voice took Chris by surprise. It also pulled him out of the game, resulting in Danny once again adding more cards to his pile.

"Look, Nanny, I'm winning." Danny grinned up at his granny who managed to produce an answering smile.

"Of course you are. You're a champion."

"And you know what?" Danny asked. "Go on, Nanny, guess."

"I don't know, Danny. Just tell me, okay."

Chris noticed how the woman struggled as she tried to

stay lighthearted for the sake of her grandson while she clearly was ready to keel over.

"Chris is going to be my trainer when I go to football." Danny grinned broadly and for just a moment his granny beamed back at him.

"Is that so? How lucky are you?" She turned to Chris. "May I?" She pointed at the seat next to him, the one Shane had vacated about an hour before.

"Of course," Chris said. "Can I get you something to drink? A cup of tea?"

"Thank you but no. If I drink anything else I may well drown. Finish your game."

Convinced that Shane's mother wanted to talk to him, Chris allowed Danny to win for the first time since they'd started playing and a few minutes later the youngster was once again the proud owner of all fifty-two cards in the deck.

"I told you he was good." The pride in her voice overrode her fatigue. "See your Uncle Shane at the bar there, Danny?" she asked.

"Yes."

"Why don't you go to him and ask him to buy you a packet of crisps. Tell him I said he should." She smiled before looking more serious. "But no more running. This is not a playground."

"Okay, Nanny."

Danny slid off his chair, abandoning the cards on the table, and they watched silently as he made his way across the pub floor as fast as he could without actually breaking into a run.

"He breaks my heart," Mrs. Boyle said when Danny reached Shane and allowed himself to be picked up. "They both do."

Chris was at a loss about how to react to the statement and kept quiet.

"Thank you," she said.

"What for?" Chris asked before realizing he sounded rude.

"I'm mean, you're welcome, but I haven't done anything."

"For catching the boy before he ran into that waitress, for keeping him occupied so he couldn't get disruptive and for somehow relieving some of Shane's stress."

Huh? Chris had no idea what she meant but was disinclined to ask.

She turned to him, her gaze fixed on his. "I'm his mother. I think I know him better than anybody else does, especially now that my..." Her words trailed off and for a moment she looked completely lost.

"I've never met you before but I saw how much it meant to Shane that you're here. I know I have no right to ask this, and maybe it's completely inappropriate but it would mean so much if you could continue to be there for him."

"Mrs. Boyle—"

"Call me Kathleen," she said.

"Kathleen, I'll do what I can to help Shane but I'm not convinced he wants me around for that." *Or for anything else.*

"Wanting you around and admitting that he wants you to be there are two very different things," Kathleen said. "He has always approached life as something he has to fight his way through on his own. I'm sure it has to do with his father leaving when he was seven and with Danny's father disappearing as soon as he discovered Ann..." She choked on the name. "That bastard left the moment Ann told him she was pregnant."

Chris was torn between delight at this opportunity to learn more about Shane and discomfort about all the private information he was getting from a woman who really didn't know him at all.

"He'd kill me if he knew I was telling you this." Clearly Kathleen was also aware of the unconventional turn their conversation had taken. "Shane's spent his adult life pushing people away and I have no doubt he'll try and do the same to you. I'm asking you to stick around despite that. He needs...friends even if he refuses to admit it."

The short hesitation before she said *friends* didn't escape Chris but he refused to attach any meaning to it.

"I'll do my best," he said. "But I can't make him accept my company or assistance."

"I know." Kathleen studied her son for a few moments. "There are times I wished he was still a child and I could force him to behave sensibly. But he's made up his mind that everybody will at some point desert him and decided he might as well push them away first." She turned to face Chris. "Can I have your phone number?"

What the...? "Of course." He rattled the numbers off when Kathleen extracted a phone from her bag.

"Thank you. I'll call you when things have settled down some. Maybe you'll have dinner with us some night?"

The hope shining in her eyes made all the excuses Chris could come up with die on his lips.

"You get on with Danny. He's clearly taken a shine to you and I can already hear him bragging to his buddies about being friends with their trainer. And like I said, even if Shane won't admit it, you're good for him. I saw how he reacted to your presence today. It helped."

Chris knew when he'd been defeated. What was more, he didn't want to give up on Shane.

"Sure," he said, "give me a call. I'd like to visit with you and your men."

"Thank you." Kathleen stood. "I'd better gather those men and go home. I know how these gatherings usually develop and I don't think I can cope with laughter and singing today." She bent forward and pressed her lips to Chris' cheek for a fleeting moment. "Despite the circumstances I'm happy to have met you, Chris."

Before he had a chance to reply she was gone and a few minutes later Shane waved at him before leaving the pub with his mother and nephew.

Chris approached the bar, captured a stool and ordered another pint. He tried to make sense of everything that had happened over the past few hours but ended up with more questions than answers. The only thing he knew for sure was that he might just have signed himself up for a complicated and potentially painful future.

The atmosphere around him changed. Just as Kathleen had predicted and in line with what he remembered from the day of his grandmother's funeral, people got louder as they ingested more alcohol. Bursts of laughter reached his ears and while Chris knew it was just another form of stress relief the sound felt tasteless and made him angry.

Irish funerals. I'll never get used to them.

He picked up his glass, drained the remaining half of his lager in one gulp and hurried out of the pub. *Maybe I'll be able to make sense of today once I'm home.* The thought was nice but he didn't hold his breath.

Chapter Fourteen

"Give us a smile."

Danny grinned straight at Shane who snapped two pictures with his phone while trying hard to keep his emotions in check. What was it about putting a child in a school uniform for the first time that made it herald the beginning of the end of their childhood?

"Take a photo of my backpack and lunch box too," Danny demanded and Shane smiled as he followed the order. The boy was so very proud of his Spiderman accessories. Combined with his excitement about going to school for the first time, his enthusiasm was contagious and under any other circumstances today would have been one of those that created memories to cherish for life. Shane didn't know what it would be like for the boy in the long term but he knew he'd always remember this day for what didn't happen, for who wasn't there more than for the momentous occasion it was.

"Is it time yet?" Danny was all but jumping up and down and raring to go.

"Almost. We'll go as soon as your granny knocks on the door." Shane checked the time. "Any minute now. Are you sure you have everything?"

It was, of course, a nonsensical question. Shane had triple-checked both Danny's bag and his lunch box, making sure he had his pencil case, books, copies and snacks.

He'd visited the school yesterday to talk to the headmistress and the very young-looking man who would be Danny's teacher for his first year in school. He'd explained the boy's circumstances to them and asked for patience and understanding in case he played up. The meeting had somewhat reassured him but he still worried they were moving too fast. Maybe it would be better to keep Danny at home for a few more days. Only a week had passed since the funeral. It was one thing for Shane to have to go back to work—he was an adult and supposed to be in control of his emotions, even if he wasn't convinced about the truth in that assertion these days. Danny, on the other hand, kept on forgetting his mother wasn't coming back and Shane could only hope his educators would deal with that in an appropriate and understanding way.

A short knock on the front window shook Shane out of his doubts and worries as Danny ran to the door, opened it and jumped straight into his granny's arms.

"Are you ready, pet?" His mother's voice sounded steady and to a casual observer she'd appear calm and relaxed, but Shane knew better. He saw the circles under her eyes, the twitch in her eye and the tension in her body. Thankfully Danny was oblivious, too caught up in his excitement to pick up on the emotional vibes surrounding him.

"Yes! Are we going now?" The boy couldn't stand still as he shifted his gaze from Shane to his granny and back again, his impatience to get going all too clear.

"Let's go." Shane closed and locked the front door before leaning in to his mother and kissing her cheek. "Are you okay?"

She shrugged in a noncommittal manner. Of course she wasn't. Just as he was anything but fine. It shouldn't be him and his mother bringing Danny to school on his first day. The only blessing right now was the fact that the boy himself hadn't picked up on the fact that the absence of the person who should be accompanying him was looming large. Whether that would still be true when they reached the school and encountered all the other new kids and their parents remained to be seen and it was a question Shane dreaded discovering the answer to.

The adults walked in silence as Danny skipped between

them, rattling off questions.

Five minutes later they strolled through the gates to the school playground. Kids ran around while their parents watched, mostly with emotional and nostalgic expressions on their faces.

Mr. McGowan, the teacher Shane had met a day earlier, stepped out of the school and clapped his hands. "Okay children, *line* please."

Most of the youngsters appeared to have no idea what they were supposed to do but enough of them understood the word for a more or less orderly line to form. Shane copied the other parents and pulled out his phone, capturing pictures of the moment for posterity. No matter that the day wasn't unfolding as it should, it was a big moment in young Danny's life and Shane would make sure he'd have the images to remember it by.

He avoided looking at his mother, knowing that if he was struggling to keep it together it had to be even harder for her. Only when the children had been herded into the building did he turn to her, studying her face. Tears swam in her eyes and Shane was torn between pretending he didn't see them and pulling her into his arms. His mother made up his mind for him when she turned and marched out of the yard, leaving him to fall into step with her.

"Do you think he'll be all right?" Shane asked.

"Yeah, I do." She turned to him and Shane recognized that while she was hurting, she didn't appear to be worried. "Kids are far better at compartmentalizing than adults are. He'll be too caught up in all the new experiences to fully realize what he's missing."

Shane said nothing. He'd known that before he asked the question, but the certainty didn't stop him from worrying.

"I mean it. He'll be fine." Clearly his mother could read Shane as easily as he could read her. "And if, God forbid, he isn't they've got my number and I'll go and get him. Don't stress about it." She stopped walking on the corner of the street. "It's your first day back in work as well. Concentrate on getting through that, I'll take care of our lad."

Shane dreaded going into VikInk. He hadn't talked to any of his colleagues since the funeral, apart from a quick call to Barry to say he'd be back today after he'd dropped Danny off at school. Part of him was glad he'd have the distraction of the job he loved to stop him obsessing about his sister, Danny and his own future. Another part worried he wouldn't be able to deal with the sympathy he was bound to receive, that his work mates' well-meaning interest in how he was managing would only make him more aware of his loss.

"I know you will," Shane said. "It's just..."

She put her hand on his arm and squeezed. "It will be like that for a while. But we'll manage. We have to." She gazed into his eyes before looking away, almost as if she felt shy.

"Please don't be angry with me."

For reasons he didn't understand, Shane suddenly felt nervous. "Why? What have you done?"

"I called that friend of yours, Chris."

"What? How? Why?" He stared at his mother and wondered if he even knew the woman standing in front of him. "How do you even know his number?"

Her lips curved into a small smile. "I asked him for it, you dope."

"And why did you contact him?"

The smile vanished again. "I've invited him for dinner tonight."

What the fuck? He knew better than to say the words out loud.

"Despite the circumstances, today is a milestone moment in Danny's life and I want to celebrate it as such. He liked Chris when he met him last week and I thought..." She stopped talking for a moment before visibly squaring her shoulders. "Having someone else with us tonight will be good. It will mean we won't be able to concentrate on who is missing as much. Chris clearly likes you, Danny took to him like a house on fire and I was quite impressed with what I saw when I talked to him. So I invited him and he said he'd come." For the first time since she'd started on this conversational line she didn't avoid his scrutiny. "And you're going to get on board with this and not put a spanner in the works."

Various reasons why this was the worst idea his mother had ever had occurred to Shane, but he kept them to himself. His mother had clearly made up her mind and she was right about Chris and Danny getting on well. And if Chris was going to be Danny's football coach there was no harm in them getting closer. Putting his foot down and insisting she uninvite him would be selfish, but shit! As if he didn't have enough to worry about right now.

He'd only been able to stop himself from obsessing about going back to work on Thursday, when Chris would also be working in VikInk, by concentrating on getting everything right for Danny's big adventure. Now he not only had to figure out how he'd get through his working day but also how he'd deal with Chris infiltrating more of his life.

"You need to get a move on."

Only when his mother said the words did Shane realize they'd been standing on the corner for at least a few minutes without either of them saying a word.

"I'll see you tonight. Just make sure you bring your friend home with you." She stretched and kissed his cheek. "It will be all right. Don't worry about it. Trust me, I'm your mother."

Still lost for words, Shane returned his mother's kiss and strode away, worry that this might well be one occasion when mother did *not* know best churning in his stomach.

* * * *

VikInk had been open for an hour when Shane arrived and business was in full swing. He took a moment to stop and study the place. It was good to be back at work. He loved his job and he mostly liked his colleagues. His gaze fell on Chris who was once again working in the station next to where Shane would be wielding his gun shortly. His back was turned toward Shane and he took advantage of the fact that he hadn't been noticed yet to study him.

Now that it really didn't matter anymore he could admit how attracted he was to the big Aussie. He'd probably been a fool. He should have taken advantage of Chris' interest in him before Ann died. Now it was too late. Even if Chris didn't mind having a fling with a man who came burdened with a child, Shane had no intention of bringing partners into Danny's life only for them to disappear again. If every child needed a stable environment to grow up in, Danny needed it more than most right now. Shane's feelings and needs would have to take a backseat for the next ten years at least. It wouldn't be easy, but he could do it. For Danny. For Ann.

"There you are!" Barry looked up from the paperwork he'd been studying behind his counter and waved him over. "It's good to have you back. How're you doing?" He scrutinized Shane.

"Not too bad," Shane replied, wondering why people kept on asking him that question and what sort of an answer they expected from him. He couldn't imagine they wanted to actually hear how hard he found every single hour of every single day right now, just as he knew they wouldn't believe him if he told them he was fine. If he'd anything to say about it those automatic, supposedly polite questions would be forbidden.

"I wanna have a word with you. Come, we'll have a coffee." Barry stepped away from the counter and led the way to the kitchen. Worry churned in Shane's stomach as he followed him. *What now? I don't need more complications.* He kept his eyes fixed on Barry's back to avoid glancing over at Chris but could still feel the man's gaze boring into him.

"Are you sure you're ready to start working again?" Barry handed Shane a mug of coffee as he asked the question before leaning against the counter and taking a sip from his own cup.

"Yeah," Shane said. "I'm good to go. Sitting at home only makes things worse, especially now Danny's started school."

It was of course the understatement of the year. Living in his sister's house surrounded by her stuff was fucking hard. His mother living next door and always being available for him and Danny made his life a lot easier of course, but his evenings were a nightmare. As soon as Danny fell asleep the walls seemed to close in on Shane. Everything he saw, used and touched had been bought or made by Ann. If it wasn't for the fact that he didn't want to rob Danny of his familiar surroundings and precious memories, he'd strip the house and give it a complete make-over.

Barry nodded. "Okay, as long as you're sure. If it turns out to be too hard, just say the word. I can't say it will be easy, but if you need to take more time, we'll manage." He sounded borderline apologetic about being nice.

"Thanks, I appreciate it."

"I've changed your hours around. As requested you now have most weekends off, although I can't promise I'll never need you to come in."

"I understand. It's not that I need to keep all my weekends free. I just want to be able to spend time with the boy and not burden my mother with him all the time. I know she'll never resent minding him but she does deserve a life of her own too."

"Good." Barry looked relieved, as if he'd been dreading this talk. "I'm sure the practicalities will work themselves out as we go." He studied the clock hanging over the kitchen door. "Your first appointment is in ten minutes. Finish your coffee and then set up." He put his cup in the sink. "Oh, before I forget, you're on a late lunch break. I've got somebody coming in for you at quarter past one."

Relief flooded Shane when he realized that meant he wouldn't have an opportunity to spend one-on-one time with Chris until after the parlor closed again. He knew he was being stupid. If he knew Chris at all he would be kind, undemanding and understanding just as he'd been the night Shane had slept in his bed. And that time he hadn't even known there was a need to be patient. Deep down inside Shane knew he could trust Chris, but that didn't make his feet feel any less heavy when he approached his station.

"Hey." Chris diverted his attention from the tattoo he was working on. "It's good to see you. It just isn't the same without you working next to me."

Bless you. Shane had no idea how Chris could possibly know not to ask him how he was doing, but the fact that he hadn't filled him with gratitude.

Before Shane could come up with a reply Barry led his first client for the day to his station. As Shane concentrated on his work his pain and worries slipped into the background for the first time since Ann had died.

Chapter Fifteen

The day felt endless, almost as if time were moving backward. Chris had been excited about seeing Shane again while also worrying about how to approach him. What could he possibly say that he hadn't already said during the funeral? He still remembered all too well how much he'd resented the well-meaning and polite but also hurtful and useless questions people had thrown at him after his grandmother's death and was determined not to pester Shane with platitudes.

He added the last detail to the small butterfly he'd inked on the shoulder of the woman currently in his chair and switched his machine off.

"There you go." He gave her the opportunity to study the work he'd done in the mirror and was gratified to see the delighted smile on her face before he covered the tattoo and sent her on her way to the counter to pay Barry.

And that, at last, was the working day over. He glanced over at Shane who was finishing a drawing in the far corner of the shop. He couldn't believe they'd managed to barely say three words to each other while working side by side all day.

He sprayed his machine with disinfectant before putting it in its case. Nerves churned through his body as he cleaned his working area, forcing himself not to look at Shane again.

He shouldn't have accepted Kathleen's dinner invitation. Not without talking to Shane first anyway. Clearly the man wasn't comfortable being around him right now. Chris had no idea what he had done to cause the sudden coolness between them and knew it didn't necessarily have anything to do with him at all. He just wasn't sure how he was supposed to spend an evening being sociable with someone who clearly didn't want to interact with him.

"Are you right?"

Chris spun around. In his determination not to stare at Shane he'd completely missed the moment he had stopped working and approached him.

"Yeah, I'm good to go." He entered the little hall leading to the kitchen and retrieved his bag. He put his tattoo machine into it, shrugged on his jacket and turned to face Shane. "Just give me a minute."

He approached the counter where Barry waited for him.

"Thank you. You've no idea how much you've helped," Barry said, holding out his hand to shake Chris'.

"You're welcome," Chris replied. "Provided Troy has no problem with it I'd be happy to do it again if you need me."

Barry grimaced. "I owe you and Troy big time. Let him know I'd be happy to return the favor should he ever need help. If you hang around for a minute I'll buy you a pint."

"Sorry," Chris said. "I've got plans. Can I take a rain check?"

"Sure, drop in if you're ever in the neighborhood." Barry slapped him on the shoulder before they shook hands again and Chris turned, expecting to see Shane behind him only to discover he was nowhere in sight.

Now what? If Shane had left without him he'd have to call Kathleen and ask for directions to her house. Of course, Shane abandoning him would be the ultimate way of letting Chris know he didn't want him to come for dinner. Maybe this was why he'd not actively pursued relationships. Was anybody worth the hassle?

He walked out of VikInk determined to call Kathleen and make his excuses. He'd no intention of showing up for a dinner at which he obviously wasn't wanted by at least one person. He also didn't want to add to what had to be a heavy burden of stress for Shane.

He pulled his phone from his pocket without checking his

surroundings and scrolled through his contacts.

"We should probably get going." Shane's voice took him by surprise. "Me ma will have dinner ready to go as soon as we walk through the door, seeing how Danny can't stay up too long. He's back in school tomorrow and bound to be tired after his first day." Shane didn't look Chris in the face as he spoke, staring over his shoulder instead.

Chris studied the phone in his hand before looking at Shane again. "If you don't want me to come, just say the word and I'll call your mother to tell her I can't make it."

Shane flinched. "Please don't. She'd have my guts for garters."

"Not if I tell her something unexpected came up," Chris said. "You're clearly not happy with me, or about me coming for dinner. I don't particularly want to spend my evening where I'm not wanted."

Much to Chris' surprise Shane blushed and appeared embarrassed. "Don't. You're not unwanted." He took off, as if it was easier to talk while he didn't have to also face Chris. "I just don't think I'm good company right now and I can't imagine spending the night with an over-excited five year old, a grief-stricken granny and moody me is your idea of a fun and relaxing evening."

Chris fell into step next to Shane and said nothing for a moment while he tried to figure out what it was Shane wasn't saying. Did he think Chris was expecting a night of wild sex just because he'd been invited to a family dinner? Not that he was inclined to ask *that* question.

"That's not an issue," he said after deciding to take Shane's words literally rather than guess at any hidden meanings. "I liked Danny and your mother when I met them last week. You may have noticed I enjoy spending time with you. I'm not sacrificing an evening to do you, or your mother for that matter, a favor."

Shane glanced at him, opened his mouth and closed it again without saying a word. A few minutes later they turned onto O'Connell Street.

"We can get a bus here," Shane said, "but it's just as fast to walk."

The evening was pleasant and dry while the lines of people waiting at the bus stops were long.

"I'm good with a walk," Chris replied as he scrambled for a way to alleviate the tension between them before they reached their destination. He didn't want to put more pressure on Shane who was coping with enough without Chris adding to the burden. On the other hand, if he didn't ask for clarification, the question would just continue to hang between them, only adding to the tense atmosphere. He took a deep breath.

"What's up? You've been avoiding me very successfully all day despite the fact that we worked next to each other. Did I do something to upset you? Should I have stayed away from the funeral last week?"

"What? Fuck! No!" Shane stared straight ahead as he almost shouted the words. "It was good to see you there and you've no idea how much I...we appreciated the time you spent with Danny. This, my mood, has very little to do with you except..."

Chris waited for Shane to finish what he'd started to say. He silently counted from one to twenty in his head before concluding that he wouldn't get to hear the rest unless he pressed for it.

"Except what?" He asked eventually.

"You...I...bollix." He muttered the last word under his breath. "I don't know what to do with you."

"You don't have to do anything with me." Chris suppressed the urge to say something flippant.

Shane stopped walking and turned to face Chris. "We're nearly there and I want to get this out of the way before we get home." He took a deep breath and swallowed so hard his Adam's apple visibly bobbed up and down. "There's something between us. I can feel it and I'm sure you can too."

Chris nodded.

"And I can't do anything with that now. The timing is wrong. I don't have the time for a fling, my life doesn't accommodate pick-ups and hot sex anymore." He smirked. "We should have taken the opportunity when I slept in your house. That way we would have dealt with the sexual tension between us and it wouldn't be an issue now. But since we didn't and it is, I need you to know that whatever might have happened died with my sister."

Chris swallowed the angry outburst burning on his tongue. He hated that Shane only thought of him in terms of a hook-up. Then he remembered the description of Shane that Troy and Xander had provided him with and what Kathleen had said about her son and the puzzle pieces fell into place. This was where he was supposed to stop Shane from pushing him away. He could only think of one way to do that. Complete honesty had never scared him as much in the past.

He stepped closer to Shane, keeping his gaze fixed on Shane's eyes, which widened in wonder before he stepped back until the wall behind him stopped his retreat. Using his length and bulk to his advantage, Chris towered over Shane, placing a hand on the wall next to Shane's head before bending forward and pressing his lips against Shane's. The kiss was short and harsh. When Chris pulled back Shane opened his mouth to say something, and Chris was fairly sure he knew what that would be, but he spoke first.

"I am not interested in a hook-up. I'm not stupid enough to expect you to flirt with me in front of your mother, never mind a five year old. I *am* very interested in you. I like you. I've enjoyed the time we spent together and I would like more of that. No. Strings. Attached."

Shane stared at him without saying a word.

"Let's go. We don't want to keep your mother waiting."

"Right." Shane pushed away from the wall, turned the corner and led them a few doors down the street before knocking on a window.

* * * *

"Will you have some more?" Kathleen picked up the serving spoon and reached for Chris' plate.

"I've already had two helpings." Chris laughed. "Your shepherd's pie is amazing, Kathleen, but, honestly, I couldn't eat another bite."

"Not even dessert?" Danny asked. "Can I have yours?"

"Danny!" both Shane and Kathleen said at the same time.

"If he doesn't want it…" Danny pouted.

Chris settled back in his chair and observed the family dynamic, enjoying the way these three people interacted. Danny had regaled them with excited tales about his first day at school ever since Shane and Chris had walked through the front door. His teacher was cool, the other kids were great and he couldn't wait to go again. The only thing he wasn't impressed with was the fact he still didn't know how to read. "But I did draw a cool picture," Danny said.

"What did you draw?" his granny asked.

"I'll show you." Danny slipped off his chair.

"Danny!" Shane's voice was soft but there was a clear warning in it.

"Sorry," Danny said. "May I be excused?"

"Sure, go ahead, pet," Kathleen said with a smile.

The boy ran off, returning moments later with a piece of paper in his hand. "Look, I drew Mammy. In Heaven."

It was as if all the air had been sucked out of the room. Nobody said a word while both Kathleen and Shane struggled to keep their composure.

"Show me." Chris held out his hand, took the paper from Danny and placed it on the table in front of him. "Come here, tell me about it."

Danny came to stand next to him and pointed. "That's God," he said, pointing at a stick figure with a huge beard. "That's Mammy, but she has wings 'cause now she's an angel."

Chris nodded.

"And that," Danny continued.

"Is a rainbow," Chris said, finishing the sentence for the boy.

"Yes, because the rainbow is like a bridge and Mammy waits there until I'm ready to go to Heaven too."

Chris almost smiled at the mixture of after-death theories the boy had created, but once he thought about it he realized it made sense. After all, if pets waited for their owners at the rainbow bridge, why wouldn't parents wait for their kids there too? As ideas went, this was probably the most comforting he'd ever heard.

"Excuse me for a moment." Kathleen sounded choked up as she stood and collected the dinner plates before carrying them to the kitchen.

"Do you like it?" Danny asked, looking up at Chris with large, hope-filled eyes.

"I think it's perfect," Chris said, meaning it exactly as he said it.

"So do I." Shane sounded like he was struggling as well and Chris ached to reach out and comfort him, the knowledge that the gesture would more than likely not be welcomed only just restraining him.

"I'll think we'll put this on the fridge when we go home." Shane's statement earned him a huge grin from Danny.

"Who wants cake then?" If there was a forced note of happiness to Kathleen's voice, Danny at least didn't notice it.

They sat in silence as she cut and shared out the chocolate cake, the mood in the room suddenly catching up with Danny too, whose bottom lip quivered a bit.

"I bet you could help me, Danny," Chris said, hoping that a change of topic might lighten the atmosphere. "I need a park with a great playground. Do you know of such a place?"

"Yes!" Danny livened up again. "There's one just over there." He waved his hand over his shoulder, indicating what could be any direction. As the boy set off on a long and detailed listing of all the various apparatus available to kids there, Chris caught Shane gazing at him as if he was trying to solve a mystery.

"Why do you want to know?" Danny tilted his head. "You're too big to play there."

Chris grinned. "That's not fair. What if I wanted to crawl through those tubes?"

Danny giggled. "You'd get stuck. Like Winnie the Pooh when he eats too much honey."

"I'll tell you why I asked," Chris said. "I'm minding my goddaughter on Sunday so I thought it might be nice to take her out to play. She's almost the same age as you, so if you like it there, I think she'll enjoy it too."

Danny nodded, a serious expression on his face. "Yes. Girls like the playground too. I sometimes play with girls there."

Chris hesitated, wondering whether he'd be pushing his luck or doing exactly the right thing.

"In that case, maybe you and your uncle and granny could come too. We could have a picnic." He concentrated on Danny, afraid to look at either Shane or Kathleen in case he had gone too far.

"I'm out, I'm afraid," Kathleen said with genuine regret in her voice. "A friend is taking me to Wicklow for the day. But you could go, Shane. It'd be good for both you and Danny."

Chris held his breath, suddenly sure that if Shane said no, the playdate wouldn't be the only thing he was rejecting.

Chapter Sixteen

Bastard.

Shane made a point of staring at the slice of chocolate cake in front of him. He took a bite, although his appetite had vanished, to give himself a few moments to collect his thoughts.

He knew exactly what Chris was doing. He was making a point, telling Shane that the presence of Danny wasn't an obstacle as far as he was concerned. But that wasn't the issue. What his nephew needed in his life right now was stability, people who would stay around, be a constant in his life. Shane had no intention of allowing the lad to get attached to Chris only for the man to disappear again sometime in the probably not-too-distant future.

"An e, ucleane?"

"Not with your mouth full, Danny."

The lad swallowed the last of his cake. "Sorry, Granny." He turned to Shane. "Can we go to the park on Sunday? Please?"

Shane sighed. "Yes, we can."

The bright, almost glowing grin on Danny's face was worth all the reservations Shane had about the idea although it didn't make him feel any kinder toward Chris.

"Will you look at the time!" Kathleen sounded shocked.

Shane turned his phone on and was surprised to see it was almost eight o clock.

"Okay, munchkin. It's time for BBS."

"Not yet. I'm not tired at all." Danny puffed out his chest and yawned loudly at the same time.

"Hey," Shane said. "We talked about this. No negotiating

on school nights. Remember?"

He almost smiled when the boy visibly deflated, only stopping himself because Danny was smart enough to take advantage of any sign of weakness in the adults around him.

"Give your nanny a kiss and say goodbye to Chris. Go on."

"But I want him to read me a story." Danny pointed at Chris. "Will you read me a football story, Chris?"

"I..." Chris glanced at Shane before focusing on Danny again. "That's probably not a good idea, buster. I should go."

Shane wanted to curse when Danny dropped his chin to his chest. *This* was exactly why he'd wanted to keep Chris out of the boy's life.

He sighed and turned to Chris. "Can you stay to read him a story?"

"Sure, I'd love to."

To his credit, Shane had to admit that he believed Chris meant those words exactly as they sounded.

* * * *

Twenty minutes later, when Shane had finished mopping up the wet mess Danny's bath had turned the bathroom into, a freshly bathed Danny lay snuggled up in his bed while Chris sat on the floor next to him, taking care of the story-part of their nighttime routine. Chris' voice was soft and calming. Shane rested against the doorframe and closed his eyes. He hadn't paid much attention to it before, but Chris' accent was a funny mix of Australian and Irish. He allowed the words of the story to wash over him and didn't open his eyes until Chris said 'the end'.

The sight before him made him smile. Danny was fast asleep, sucking on his thumb. It was a habit he'd picked up shortly after Ann had been hospitalized and neither Shane nor his mother had had the heart to try to put a stop to it.

They'd have to deal with it soon, but not yet.

Chris stood up and turned to put the book back on the shelf. Shane took the opportunity to study him. He was built. Tall and broad-shouldered, he was something of a man-mountain. Shane's gaze lingered on Chris' arse and for a moment he imagined what it would be like to squeeze those globes, see them naked. Then Chris turned around and the moment was gone. Shane was still pissed off with him, great storytelling abilities and wonderful body notwithstanding.

"Let's go downstairs." Shane allowed Chris to walk past him before closing Danny's bedroom door and following him down.

Chris came to a standstill in the hall, clearly uncertain what to do next. Shane stalked toward him, stopping only when less than a meter separated them.

"Don't do that again." He didn't even try to hide the anger in his voice.

"Do what?" Confusion creased Chris' brow.

"Invite Danny to something without talking to me about it first. What if I hadn't wanted to go? What if I'd already made other plans? You had no way of knowing you weren't setting him up for a disappointment."

"Shit." Chris frowned. "Fuck but I'm stupid." He closed his eyes for a moment before meeting Shane's gaze head on. "I'm sorry. You are right. I had no way of knowing any of those things and I should have kept my big mouth shut."

Shane deflated. He'd been ready for an argument. In a way he'd been hoping for a fight. Shouting at Chris, lashing out even, might just release some of the tension curled up in his belly, smoldering away like a volcano waiting to erupt. Not to mention that it would probably end with Chris never wanting to see him again, thus solving the ridiculous issue of Shane being unable to shake his attraction to him.

"Listen, if you want me to tell Danny there's been a change of plans I'll do so. He's probably still awake." Chris took a few steps toward the stairs.

"Leave it," Shane said. "Just because you deliver the message won't mean he's any less disappointed."

"I know, but at least it would make me the bad guy rather than you."

"As it should be," Shane muttered before letting go of most of his frustration. "No, it's not a bad idea, actually. I didn't have anything planned for Sunday and it will do him good to be out and about, running off some of the never-ending supply of energy he appears to have."

Chris smiled. "Kids are something else, aren't they? I'll never know how they keep going. And why do we lose that ability to keep on running as we grow older? God knows there are days I could do with some of that resilience."

Chris certainly sounded as if he knew what he was talking about, but Shane still couldn't shake the feeling he'd been set up.

"Tell me. Is there really a goddaughter you need to mind on Sunday or do you now have to go and borrow a child somewhere?" He'd been only half serious but one quick glance at Chris told Shane he'd insulted him.

"I may say things I shouldn't say. I may need to think before I speak." Chris sounded as annoyed as he looked. "But I do not lie." Then the irritation disappeared from his features again. The understanding Shane thought he recognized in his eyes was almost harder to bear. *Damn.* He didn't want sympathy or patience. He wanted Chris to realize there was nothing to be gained for him here, that Shane had nothing to offer. He needed Chris to walk away. *So why can't I find the words to just tell him to fuck off?* Shane didn't pursue the question, fully aware that he wouldn't like the answer.

"Tell me about this goddaughter of yours." If he couldn't say what needed to be said he might as well focus on something safe.

"She's great. She's also exhausting. A combination of tomboy and she-devil is the best description I can come up with." Chris grinned, the affection he felt for the girl he was talking about obvious on his face. "She's a live-wire, that one. Don't worry, she won't have any problem keeping up with Danny. Those two might well be a match made in Heaven...or Hell, depending on their mood."

And they won't be on their own. Shane felt torn. Heaven or Hell was a good way to describe the dilemma he faced. All his instincts told him to send Chris away. He didn't need him. Chris would only complicate matters more and Shane's life felt like one long obstacle course as it was. And yet... He couldn't get the persistent little fucker of a voice in his head to shut up. The one that kept on insisting that he'd be pushing away an opportunity, a chance to find something he'd never realized he wanted, something he didn't believe existed for people like him.

"Do you want a beer?"

Chris studied him for a moment and Shane had to force himself not to look away or withdraw the offer.

"Sure, I'll have a tinny, if you're sure you don't want me to go that is."

"Sit down." Shane pointed toward the living room. "I'll grab our drinks." He turned to the kitchen without waiting to see if Chris would do as he'd suggested.

Damn the man. Why did he have to behave as if he understood Shane? Why couldn't he be unreasonable or selfish? He opened the fridge and grabbed two cans.

"Do you want a glass?" he asked without turning around.

"Nah, just the can is fine." Chris' answer was just loud enough for Shane to hear him, which meant it was unlikely the sound would carry upstairs to disturb Danny. Another mark on the plus side.

He walked into the living room to find Chris sitting on the couch, just left of the middle. Shane considered taking the armchair. It would send a clear message that he intended to keep Chris at arm's length. Except that he wasn't at all sure he really wanted to keep his distance. He was tired. Only a week had passed since Ann's funeral and Shane wasn't sure how much longer he could keep the façade up. He had to be strong—for Danny, for his ma—but when did he get to give in to the pain and doubts he wasn't able to shake? Who was going to be strong for him when he just couldn't do it anymore?

He handed a can to Chris before lowering himself to the far right corner of the couch, a weak compromise between what he wanted—to crawl onto Chris' lap and lose himself and his dark thoughts in the man for a while—and what he knew he should do—create as much distance as he could.

Shane felt Chris staring at him and tried to ignore it, but his body appeared to have a mind of its own and before he could think better of it he'd turned his head and lost himself in Chris' compassion-filled eyes.

Chris raised his arm and rested it on the top of the couch in an open and obvious invitation. "I know what you're doing," Chris said without taking his eyes off Shane. "I also know it's not a good idea."

"What's that supposed to mean?" Shane heard the aggressive note in his voice and wanted to take the words back. They weren't even true since he had a pretty good idea what Chris was getting at. But he'd said them and now he'd have to wait and see what would follow.

"When my granny died," Chris said, apparently ignoring Shane's statement, "I had this interesting conversation with Caroline. She's a former girlfriend of mine and Maya's mother."

That's right, he's bisexual. For some reason Shane had forgotten that detail about Chris. He allowed the idea to percolate for a moment before realizing that it really didn't matter.

"And?" he asked when it seemed as if Chris wasn't going to finish whatever he'd started saying.

"Sorry." Chris grimaced. "I'm just trying to figure out if there's a way of saying this without pissing you off again."

Shane winced. *I probably deserve that.* "Go on," he said. "Just spit it out. I'll behave."

"I told you my mother more or less disowned me when

I turned eighteen. So when my granny died that was basically my whole family gone. I was devastated, but I had no intention of letting others know how I felt. I didn't want pity or sympathy. So I pushed the sad away and turned angry."

Chris' gaze turned distant and unfocused, as if he no longer saw Shane but images from the past instead.

"Because she was my best friend and refused to let we wallow in my misery, Caroline took the brunt of my anger. She could have turned her back on me. I'm still not sure why she didn't, but she stuck around. She allowed me to get away with lashing out at her for a few days and then she pulled me up on it."

Despite himself and fully aware that he was being lectured to, Shane was intrigued by Chris' story. As much as he was sure it would be better if he pushed him from his life, Shane couldn't help being curious about what made Chris tick. He turned on the couch to fully face Chris, moving himself somewhat closer to him in the process.

"I'm not going to repeat everything she said. A lot of it is not relevant to your situation anyway. If only because I didn't have a child to contend with." Chris hesitated again.

"I'm not sure what is worse," Shane said, surprising himself. "Having Danny and knowing everything he's lost is hard, I'm not going to pretend it isn't. But I can't imagine what it would be like to be completely alone. No matter how hard this is I have me ma and Danny to keep me going."

Chris shrugged. "A smarter person than me once said that you can't compare suffering. We all hurt and deal with the pain in unique ways. What is the same for most of us is that we have the right to be angry and upset, that there is no shame in ranting and crying. She told me I was a fool to not take advantage of the support on offer." Chris stopped talking but his eyes asked the question his mouth didn't verbalize — *are you going to be as big a fool as I was?*

"Come here." Chris whispered the words. "Let me hold

you for a while. You don't have to be strong for me."

In the back of his mind a soft voice urged Shane to keep his distance but he ignored it—his need stronger than his fear of what giving in might mean—and closed the distance between himself and Chris, sighing in relief when Chris pulled him close until his head rested on the broad shoulder.

He closed his eyes and breathed in the comforting smell of the infuriating Aussie who wouldn't take no for an answer. The combination of detergent, aftershave and something he could only identify as pure Chris filled his senses, taking him back to the only night over the past six weeks he'd managed to get a good and restful sleep—in Chris' bed.

"That's it." Chris whispered the words into his ear as he stroked Shane's back. "Relax for a while."

I could ask him to stay. Shane pushed the thought away as soon as it crossed his mind. If Chris was still here in the morning that would only confuse Danny, create expectations that would never be fulfilled. But maybe he could allow himself to indulge for a while now. It only meant something if he attached a meaning to it.

The silence surrounding them comforted Shane. For the first time in a week he didn't feel the need to turn the television on just to distract himself from the thoughts running through his head. The thoughts and worries were still there, but they didn't feel as insurmountable right now. He knew tomorrow would be as hard as today had been. He had no doubt that would be the case for the foreseeable future, but it was okay if he didn't worry about those things morning, noon and night. He lost track of time as he surrendered to the comfort of Chris' presence and embrace.

"I should probably go."

Chris' words shook Shane from the mindless daze he'd lost himself in.

"What time is it?" he asked.

"Half ten," Chris said. "Not late, but we both have to work tomorrow and you have a little boy to deal with too."

"Yeah." Shane forced himself to sit up again, finding it much harder than he'd expected to leave the comfort of Chris' arms. "You're probably right." He stood and watched as Chris followed his example, taking notice of the small wince crossing his features when he stretched to his full length.

"Are you okay?" Shane asked.

"Grand." Chris smiled. "Just not as young and supple as I used to be, obviously."

When they got to the front door Chris turned to him and cupped his chin. "Don't push me away. I'm not the enemy. I'm not going to hurt you or your family, I promise." He bent forward and pressed his lips against Shane's before he could form a reply.

He threw caution to the wind and returned the kiss, parting his lips in the process, inviting Chris in. The encounter was sweet and comforting rather than hot and demanding. *I could get used to this.* In the past kissing had only been a means to an end, a preferably brief interlude before getting to what Shane considered the real business — getting laid. Obviously he'd been missing out. This was good. He could lose himself in these sensations. He could almost believe he was wanted, that he wouldn't be cast aside, that Chris could be trusted.

When they parted again Chris pulled his phone from his pocket. "If we're going to meet up on Sunday I'm really going to need your number."

Shane rattled the numbers off, still not entirely comfortable with Chris having them but acknowledging not giving it would be foolish.

"I'll call you on Saturday to finalize the arrangements for Sunday." Chris opened the front door. "See you then."

Shane watched Chris walk away until he rounded the corner and was gone from sight. He closed the door and leaned back against it. *What the fuck am I doing?* It was so tempting to give in and believe the fairytale. He wanted Chris to be the man who changed the pattern, the one who would stay, but Shane knew only too well that nobody ever did.

He was so very tired of doing it all by himself. Of course his mother did more than her bit when it came to minding Danny, so that part of his life was covered. But he knew he needed someone to talk to, to share his thoughts and fears with. Maybe it was because he'd been made all too aware of how fragile life was, but for the first time Shane acknowledged that going it alone would be harder than sharing the burden.

He'd compromise. As long as he could keep the closeness between him and Chris a secret from Danny and his mother, he might as well indulge in it. He'd stay alert. The moment Chris gave any signs of retreating, Shane would push him away first. He'd just need to make sure he didn't get too comfortable on those broad shoulders or too used to having Chris around.

Chapter Seventeen

"Sure, that sounds like fun."

Chris listened to Troy's side of a telephone conversation as he cleaned his working area. It was the first time since Pins & Needles had opened in the morning that he'd had a few minutes to himself. To say the day had been busy would be a gross understatement. Good news for Troy, and Chris wasn't complaining either. Constant work had left him with little or no time to obsess about Shane and the reprieve was welcome.

"Hang on a sec and I'll ask him." Troy stepped into Chris' field of vision. "Have you got plans for tonight?" Troy's question took Chris by surprise.

"Nope. I've got nothing on, why?"

"Lorcan invited Xander and me over for the evening. He said to bring you along if you were available." Troy stared at the phone in his hand. "So, are you up for it?"

"Sure," Chris said, instantly realizing that it was exactly what he needed. He could do with a break from the thoughts about Shane swirling through his head. He couldn't believe how fast the man had gotten under his skin, or how deep. He wished he understood him better. If only he could figure out what made Shane run hot one minute and cold the next, he'd be able to deal with it. Instead, Chris was playing a guessing game and he hated every second of it. And yet he knew without a shadow of a doubt that if he were to just come out and ask Shane what he wanted, it would be the end of the fragile bond they'd managed to establish.

He just needed to figure out how to get his mind to shut the fuck up for a few hours. Spending time with Troy,

Xander, Eric and Lorcan ought to do the trick and distract him for the evening.

"Good." Troy brought his phone back to his ear as he turned away from Chris and walked through the door connecting the parlor to Xander's studio, talking to Lorcan as he went.

Chris finished the clean-up and wondered what to do next when Troy joined him again. "We'll go straight from here, if that's okay with you. Eric and Lorcan are ordering in Chinese and we're to pick some cans on the way."

"Sounds like a plan to me," Chris said.

* * * *

"I meant to ask you earlier," Troy said as they walked away from Pins & Needles. "How did your last day in VikInk go?"

"It was grand," Chris replied. "Much like the other two in that I only got the simple and quick jobs, but that was to be expected."

"I bet Barry took you for a few pints afterwards. The head sore today?"

Chris laughed. "You know him well. He did offer but I had to decline."

"You had other plans?"

"Something like that." Chris wasn't comfortable discussing Shane with Troy and Xander. In fact he'd avoided the subject ever since the conversation in which he'd been told all about Shane's bad boy days.

"Oh, cagey." Xander smirked. "Secret date was it?"

Chris bristled, torn between telling them nothing and laying it all out in the hope that it would be the last time they'd have this particular conversation. Not because he feared his continued interactions with Shane would cause problems but because he really didn't want to hear all their warnings again. On the other hand, he wasn't prepared to tiptoe around them just because he worked for Troy and his partner and they'd had bad experiences with Shane.

"Nothing secret about it. Nothing overly exciting either. Shane's mother invited me over for dinner and I went."

Troy and Xander said nothing, but Chris didn't miss the way they looked at each other or the frowns on their faces.

"I didn't realize you knew his mother," Troy said eventually. "Oh, wait. You would have met her when you went to the funeral. Did you have a good night?"

"I'm not sure 'good' is the word I'd choose," Chris said. "It was hardly going to be a party after everything they've been through, but it was pleasant enough. Not as sad as I feared it might be."

"I have to say I'm amazed," Troy said.

"How's that?" Chris asked, knowing full well that he probably wouldn't like Troy's answer. But he wanted to have the subject dealt with once and for all. If he had anything to do with it he'd be seeing a lot more of Shane and he didn't want to have to keep that a secret...if it happened.

"I have a hard time coming to terms with Shane still tolerating your presence."

Chris blinked and stopped walking. *Tolerating me?* "What's that supposed to mean?"

"I'm sorry." Troy came to a halt a few paces ahead of Chris and turned to face him. "That came out wrong. It's just that if past experience is anything to go by, he should have kicked you to the curb weeks ago. I can't help feeling he's just biding his time before he pushes you away." Troy's words were harsh but Chris caught the trace of uncertainty in his voice.

"Possibly," he said. "But I'm not convinced that's it."

"It's all he's ever done. You know what they say about leopards and spots, right?"

Chris was torn between being irritated about Troy lashing out against Shane again and gratitude that his boss cared enough about him to not want to see him hurt.

"He's had more than enough opportunities to send me on my way, if that's what he wanted to do." Chris wasn't about to say so out loud, but he'd spent a good part of the previous night wondering the same thing. "I'm inclined to think he doesn't know what he wants to do with me. And I'm not about to pressure him about it. Especially not now."

"Fair enough," Troy said. "His sister dying is bound to have hit him hard."

"I know it's none of my business..." Xander gave him a sheepish smile before ploughing on. "It's just that you sound as if you're falling for him. Be careful. I'd hate for him to hurt you as he did us." He waved his hand to indicate himself and Troy.

Chris pushed his growing irritation away. *What is it with the third degree?* He liked these guys and he knew they were only looking out for him, but what he did and didn't get up to with Shane was really none of their business.

"You realize I'm a big boy now, don't you?"

His two companions sniggered. "At, what are you — six foot six? — that's hard to miss," Troy said. After a moment of silence all three of them laughed. For Chris it was as much a release of tension as a reaction to the joking remark. He had enough trouble trying to figure out what exactly was going on with Shane and how to deal with it without Troy and Xander throwing their past bad experiences into the mix every time Shane's name was mentioned.

They stopped at an off-license and picked up a collection of cans.

"How about some Aussie beer?" Xander asked Chris.

"Not for me, thanks. I can't say I miss it and I much prefer Heineken."

"Don't you think we went somewhat over the top?" Chris asked when they left the shop again, each of them carrying two bags.

"Probably." Xander laughed. "But it's good to have a choice and if it doesn't get drunk today there's always tomorrow."

"Makes sense," Chris conceded. "I just hope we don't have much further to go, these bags are already cutting into my hands."

"Yeah, you'd think somebody would have invented carrier bags that are easier to use by now, wouldn't you? But, on the upside, this is as far as we go," Troy said before ringing one of the doorbells in front of them.

Two flights of stairs later Lorcan waited for them, his front door wide open. "Great timing. The food should be here in about twenty minutes. Come in." He stepped back and allowed Troy, Xander and Chris to walk past him before closing the door.

Chris studied his surroundings. He'd never been here before. Whenever he'd met Eric and Lorcan it had either been in the pub, in Pins & Needles or in Xander and Troy's place. He liked what he saw. The place had a lived-in feel and appearance and now that he thought about it, that surprised him. He'd expected any place Eric lived in to resemble a show house, picture perfect with modern and brand new furnishings. After all, the man was a renowned interior designer. There was nothing polished or artificial about his surroundings though. This was obviously a home rather than just a place to live.

"I see you made a few changes," Troy said, addressing Lorcan.

"Yes, we did. It's all finalized now." Lorcan grinned. "The place across the hall has been turned into an office and this is where we live."

"You kept that quiet." Xander turned to Eric who shrugged.

"It all happened a bit faster than we expected. Carmel got an offer to work with a large company so we ended our partnership. I'm now officially working on my own and since we had the other apartment and the owners were willing to sell it to me, it made sense to convert it."

"I still can't believe you managed to domesticate Lorcan," Troy joked.

"Hey, I was never undomesticated." The offended scowl on Lorcan's face was spoiled by the smile tugging at his lips. "Besides, we've been more or less living together for the past six months. The only difference is that we no longer have to choose between two different beds to sleep in."

"Congratulations," Chris chipped in. "If I'd known this would be a sorta housewarming party I would have brought something more sophisticated than a few tinnies along."

Eric took the bags they'd brought with them and carried them to what Chris assumed was the kitchen while the rest of them settled in the living room.

"You're not worried about going it alone?" Xander asked when Eric returned carrying a tray with drinks.

"No. In fact, it's quite a relief to no longer have to work with Carmel. As well as we got along in college and when we first started, our styles drifted ever further apart. She's all about prestigious projects and making a name for herself. Not that there's anything wrong with that, but I'd rather concentrate on a personal touch and giving people exactly what they want rather than what I think they should want."

Chris listened to the conversation. He really didn't know Lorcan and Eric well enough to contribute much, but he liked the back and forth between the four men even if it did remind him that he had few close friends of his own.

"Did Lorcan tell you we went to Killucan last weekend?" Eric asked just as the doorbell rang.

"I'll get it." Lorcan jumped up and hurried out of the door to intercept the food.

"He's eager to get away from us," Troy said. "What's up with him? Did something happen while you were in Killucan?"

"You could say that." Eric smiled broadly. "His granny got up to her tricks again."

"Knowing the woman, that could easily have gone either way," Troy said. "I take it whatever she did worked out okay then?"

"Surprisingly well in fact." Eric grinned.

"Well, don't leave us hanging. What happened?" Xander

143

asked.

"She'd invited us to have dinner with her in this restaurant and told us not to bother picking her up because she'd make her own way there. So we arrived and walked in only to…"

The front door slammed shut and moments later, Lorcan returned to the room, carrying three carrier bags filled with containers. "I hoped you'd be done with that story by now or had at least gotten plates and cutlery ready. Jaysus, do I have to do it all?"

Chris struggled to keep up with what was going on around him. He remembered hearing something about not all of Lorcan's family accepting him being gay and in a relationship, but he had no idea about the details and wasn't sure why Eric was so delighted or why Lorcan appeared to be uncomfortable.

Eric laughed, clearly unimpressed by his boyfriend's grumblings. "Hold your horses, I'm on it." He got up and turned to the kitchen. "Anyone want another drink while I'm up?"

The next few minutes were a hustle of food containers being organized on the table and the five of them filling their plates with what appeared to be an endless variety of dishes.

"So, you walked in and…?" Troy asked after they'd all settled again.

"Why don't you tell them?" Eric looked at Lorcan with such tenderness it took Chris' breath away. *To be loved that much.*

Lorcan's cheeks turned pink as he glared at Eric.

"Turned out she'd invited my whole family." There was a strange edge to Lorcan's voice. "All of them were there, including Laura's kids." He stopped talking and concentrated on the plate on his lap.

"And?"

Lorcan continued to focus on his food for a while, putting a new forkful in his mouth as soon as he swallowed the last one.

"It was okay." He looked up from his plate and turned to Troy. "I mean, at first it was awkward as fuck. I love my granny but when I saw them all sitting there I would have lovingly strangled her." A smile tugged at his lips. "Am I horrible because I enjoyed that my parents seemed to be as uncomfortable as I felt?"

"I don't understand," Xander said. "Didn't things get better after your parents told you they'd not voted against equality in the referendum?"

"Well, that's part of the problem, isn't it? They told me but they didn't tell each other."

"And his grandmother decided that nonsense had gone on for long enough," Eric added.

Lorcan laughed out loud. "My poor parents. They didn't know what hit them when my formerly ever so docile granny put her foot down and told them that she was fed up with her family being fragmented and that it was going to end that night."

"Fair play to her." Troy sounded delighted for his friend. "And did she put a stop to it?"

"Up to a point. I don't think they're ever going to be comfortable with the idea of Eric and me."

"You don't know that." Eric interrupted his boyfriend in a tone of voice that suggested they'd had this discussion before.

Lorcan shrugged. "We'll see. I'm just glad that they've decided to be agreeable and no longer look at us as if we're the scum of the earth. Having to visit them on my own after living with you for all this time was getting old fast. I've no doubt that the first time Eric comes with me is going to be strained, but at least he will be welcomed — reluctantly or otherwise."

"Funny isn't it," Troy said. "How our parents have come around. First my father and now your parents. If anybody had told me this would happen when I was sixteen I would have told them they were crazy."

Chris zoned out of the conversation as Troy and Lorcan

went on a trip down memory lane. Maybe he should be grateful he didn't have any family in his life to be upset about who he chose to date. He knew *his* granny hadn't minded. He'd told her he was bisexual soon after first arriving in Ireland. At the time he'd figured he might as well get it out of the way before they could grow close since he'd fully expected her to not understand at best or be appalled at worst. She'd surprised him by saying all she wanted was for him to be happy. Of course he had no way of knowing what his mother's reaction might have been if he'd ever had the opportunity to tell her. As it was, she'd disappeared from his life before he'd figured it out for himself so it had never been an issue.

He finished his dinner, thoughts and memories running through his mind and absentmindedly accepted another can from Lorcan.

"That's a somewhat touchy subject." For some reason Troy's words registered with Chris and he forced his attention back to the conversation flowing around him only to find four pairs of eyes fixed on him.

"What?" He looked down to inspect his clothing, worried he'd managed to spill food all over himself.

"Eric suggested that we'd have to set you up with someone to even out the numbers," Xander said.

"Oh." Chris wasn't sure what, if anything, to say about that. *Fuck it.* He might as well force the issue and find out exactly where he stood.

"You mean that I could only bring a boyfriend along if you all approve of him?" He kept his tone of voice neutral. He wanted clarification, not a fight.

"Of course not," Eric laughed. "What has your choice of partner to do with us?"

"So if I wanted to bring Shane along to an evening like this that would be okay?" Chris studied the can in his hand, suddenly worried he'd gone too far.

"Shane?" Lorcan asked. "*That* Shane?"

"The one and only," Troy said before turning to Chris.

146

"It would be okay. It would be awkward as fuck, and I'm not convinced Shane would be any more comfortable with the situation than Xander or me, but if the two of you do end up in a relationship—as unlikely as I think that is—we wouldn't turn you or him away."

Chris stared at Troy, searching his face for hidden meanings. Finding none, he relaxed. His boss was right of course. He couldn't imagine Shane being at ease in the company of Troy and Xander either, but given that he had no idea whether or not Shane would be interested in a relationship, that wasn't something he needed to worry about. Right now he just relished the fact that Troy and his friends thought highly enough of him to put their own dislikes aside should he and Shane ever get it together.

"Thank you. I can't see it happening anytime soon, if ever, but it's good to know it won't be an issue if it does."

After all, stranger things have happened. Look at Lorcan and his family. Deep inside Chris, a tiny seed of hope sprouted its first tendrils. On Sunday he'd spend another day with Shane, albeit while chaperoned by two rug rats, and he had truly been accepted as a friend by his employer and his mates. He'd focus on the positives and deal with any issues as they arose.

Chapter Eighteen

"Is it time yet?" Danny bounced up and down while trying to squirm his way between Shane and the kitchen counter, making it all but impossible for Shane to get the sandwiches for their picnic made.

"Almost, and if you just let me get on with it, we'd go that much sooner. Have you got your football?" He took himself by surprise sometimes. He'd never been known for his patience and yet where Danny was concerned it came to him automatically.

Danny retreated a few steps, allowing Shane to pull containers from the cabinet. "Did you talk to Chris? Are you sure he's going to be there? Do you think he'll play football with me? Do girls like football?"

"Do you ever breathe?" Shane stared at his nephew in wonder.

"That's silly." Danny laughed. "Everybody breathes."

Shane put the now-filled containers into his backpack and went over his mental check list. He had enough food to feed all four of them if necessary, and he had an extra set of clothes for Danny in case he managed to destroy the ones he was wearing. He thought for a moment, sure there was something else he should be bringing, while Danny ran around like an excited foal, all uncoordinated and wild. When the boy tripped over the rug and nearly fell he knew exactly what he needed. He entered the bathroom, pulled out the first-aid box and extracted plasters and disinfectant — better to be safe than sorry.

"Can we go now?" Danny didn't even try to hide his impatience.

Shane laughed. "Yes, we're ready." Danny was at the front door before he finished the sentence.

The next five minutes were a battle of wills between Danny, who would have run all the way to the park given half a chance, traffic be damned, and Shane. He remembered making the same journey with Ann and Danny before going to America and wondering how his sister did it. At the time he'd thought that raising a child had to be the most exhausting and possibly frustrating job in the world. Now he *knew* it was indeed very tiring, but rather than being frustrating he found the whole experience surprisingly rewarding. The boy never ceased to amaze him. Danny had the power to make him smile and laugh at a time when he didn't think he'd ever do so again. The unconditional love the boy bestowed on Shane took his breath away. When Ann had first asked him to be the boy's guardian he'd been afraid he'd end up resenting Danny, but that fear had evaporated. Shane's life had been far less complicated before Danny, but it had also been empty and he'd been a selfish bastard.

As soon as they walked through the gates to the park Danny was off, running for the playground as if his life depended on it. The fact that they'd almost arrived at their destination had the opposite effect on Shane and he slowed down. He needed to come to a decision about Chris. It might have seemed like a good idea to just allow him to hang around while Shane kept him at arm's length, but after thinking about little else for the past two days and nights he had to admit that it was in fact no plan at all.

He came to the edge of the field with the playground and saw that Danny had already found Chris and the little girl, who'd claimed one of the picnic tables surrounding the playground. Shane watched as the two kids eyed each other as if trying to figure out what they were dealing with. The moment was over almost before it had begun and they were off to the slide, giggling as they went.

When Chris turned around and looked at him, Shane's

heart fluttered and he couldn't stop himself from smiling. *Yeah. So much for keeping my distance.* He refused to acknowledge the mild panic surging in his stomach as he crossed the field.

"Hey." Shane forced a calm he didn't feel into his voice. "I see you got here early too."

Chris groaned. "I probably shouldn't have told Maya about this outing as soon as her parents dropped her off. She's been at me to come here for the past two hours. In the end it seemed easier to just go and arrive early."

Shane laughed. "Yeah, I'm taking a crash course in parenting too. The little bugger had me up at six and has been pestering me since. Even his favorite TV shows couldn't distract him."

"Just goes to show how little I know. It never even occurred to me to suggest television to Maya."

Shane shrugged his backpack off and put it underneath the table before sitting down. "I'm fairly sure most experts agree that allowing kids too much screen time isn't a good idea, but I have to admit that it can be a blessing when I need a few minutes of uninterrupted time."

Chris sat next to him, opened a large bag and extracted a Thermos flask and two plastic mugs. "Coffee?"

"You're a lifesaver. I knew I was forgetting something." Shane gratefully accepted the cup when Chris passed it to him.

A shriek from the playground almost made Shane drop his drink.

"Danny! Take it easy." Shane stared in horror at his nephew pushing the swing with the little girl on it. Not only was she going higher than he was comfortable with, she also swung violently from left to right. Just as well the swings on either side of her were unoccupied.

"Higher! Higher!" The little girl's excitement was clear in her voice.

"I think I'd better supervise." Chris got up and stalked over to what looked like a disaster in the making to Shane.

Lifting his coffee to his mouth, Shane allowed himself to indulge in the sight of Chris. He had no idea how he'd managed to get under his skin. He'd been fighting the attraction he'd felt and had been sure it would fade. He felt a stab of guilt that he could even contemplate allowing Chris into his life so soon after Ann's death. He was supposed to be mourning, not planning a possibly happy future. And yet...

He smiled before pulling his phone from his pocket and taking a few pictures when Chris pushed two swings at the same time, making both Danny and Maya squeal with delight.

For the first time since he'd met Chris, Shane allowed himself to indulge in the fantasy. He imagined having both Danny and Chris in his life and what it would be like to share the responsibility of raising the boy. Only a few days ago he'd had the discussion with his mother. At the time he'd discarded her words as nonsense, but maybe he'd been the one to get it wrong.

'You have to stop pushing people away, son.' He could still see the worry that had been etched into her face and hear the concern in her voice. 'There's no reason why you have to do this alone, why you have to stop living.'

'Give me a break, ma.' It had been very hard to keep a handle on his temper and not take all his frustration and worry out on the woman who was only trying to help. 'Danny is my priority now and he will be until he's ready to strike out on his own. I'm not going to upset his life even more, he's been through enough.' He saw the pain in his mother's eyes and continued regardless. 'It's bad enough that he's probably the only kid in his class not living with at least one of his parents. Imagine what it would be like for him if the two people taking care of him were both male. And it's not as if I'm ever going to end up in a relationship with a woman.'

The anger flashing across his mother's face took him by surprise. 'Stop talking rubbish," she said, censure as clear in her tone of voice as it had been in her choice of words. 'You think it would do him any good to be raised by a lonely and bitter uncle? Of *course you need to put the boy first, but that doesn't mean you have to stop living. Do you think Ann gave up on the idea of a future relationship just because she had Danny? And don't you dare use being gay as an excuse. Sure, there will be people who frown upon a child being raised by a same sex couple. But then there will always be those who'll find fault. Especially after the referendum it wouldn't be anywhere near as noteworthy as you seem to think.'*

He'd known she was right while they had the conversation, even if he hadn't been inclined to admit as much. But he wasn't about to tell his mother that he wasn't sure if he was capable of relationships. He'd never given them a second thought. It had never made sense to go through the hassle of tying himself to one person when every night he went out presented itself as a human buffet. Past experience had taught him people rarely if ever stuck around, so investing time and emotions in them had always felt like a fool's errand.

"Penny for them?"

Shit. He'd been so lost in his thoughts he hadn't even noticed Chris returning.

"Trust me. You don't want to know," Shane said, unprepared to share his thoughts and feelings with Chris.

Chris sat next to him again. It could have been Shane's imagination but he was sure he was closer now than he had been earlier. Surely their thighs hadn't been touching before Chris went to deal with the kids?

"That's where you're wrong," Chris said, his voice serious and soft. "I do want to know about you and what you think."

Right. Even if Shane believed that, he wouldn't be inclined to let Chris know what had been going on in his head. Especially not with two kids around who would more than likely interrupt any conversation they might start.

As if to prove Shane right, Danny and Maya ran up to the table.

"We wanna play football," Maya announced.

"Sure," Shane said. "Danny brought a ball, so on you go."

"No, you have to play with us." Danny indicated both Chris and Shane.

Shane turned to Chris, who shrugged.

"Fair enough." Shane got up. "We'll play and then we'll have lunch. How's that?"

"Sounds like a plan," Chris said as he got up again too. "Okay, kiddos, here's how we're going to do this."

Shane listened as Chris explained the rules to what sounded like a football version of piggy-in-the-middle to Danny and Maya and grinned when he realized how clever the idea was. The kids would be doing all the running, tiring themselves and each other out, while he and Chris could more or less stand still while kicking the ball back and forth.

Forty-five minutes later they returned to the table. For the first time since they'd arrived in the park the two kids were quiet and not vying for the adults' attention. Sunlight filtered through the branches of the tree behind the picnic table, creating a mesmerizing pattern of light and shadow and keeping the temperature comfortable but not too hot. It wouldn't be long now before autumn kicked in and Shane was grateful that Chris had more or less forced him into taking advantage of what might well turn out to be one of the last days of summer.

Chris burst out laughing once both he and Shane had taken the food they'd packed for lunch from their bags. "We've got enough here to feed a family of eight. Clearly we'll need to coordinate better the next time we do this."

Shane concentrated hard on opening his containers and cartons of juice while trying not to grin. The fact that Chris was already thinking of doing this again shouldn't make him feel as good as it did, but he couldn't deny the warm glow the thought left him with.

He listened to the kids bicker over what to eat and which sandwich was the best. The discussion threatened to turn into an argument when both Maya and Danny decided they wanted the last Nutella sandwich, and Shane took the easy option and split it evenly down the middle.

"Wanna play house?" Maya asked Danny.

Shane held his breath. House didn't sound like the sort of game his boisterous nephew would go for but the boy surprised him by agreeing before running off with Maya.

"Not bad," Chris said. "Twenty minutes of peace and quiet is more than I figured we'd get."

"Tell me about it," Shane agreed. "I'd love to know the secret of where kids get their energy. I'm exhausted just trying to keep track of Danny most the time." He laughed.

"It can't be easy." Chris ignored Shane's attempt at levity and sounded serious. "You're more or less raising that kid on your own. And you were just thrown into the middle of it. Most parents get used to the job from the moment the baby is born. You didn't have that."

Shane was stunned. He hadn't figured that part of it out for himself yet, but as soon as Chris said it Shane knew he'd been right. He didn't want the man's pity though.

"It's not that bad." He put as much nonchalance in his voice as he could. "I'm not entirely on my own. My mother does a fair bit."

"Sure, but most couples with kids have grandparents to help them too. Just because your mother does her part doesn't change the fact that you *are* on your own and new to this child raising thing."

"I never thought I'd end up with a child." Shane had no idea where the words came from.

"And I always figured I would," Chris said. "Yet here I am, thirty-five years old and as far removed from fatherhood as I ever was."

The regret in Chris' voice took Shane's breath away. It also confused him.

"But it's not too late for you. You're bisexual. If you hook up with a woman you could solve that problem in about nine months."

Chris stared at Shane as if he'd lost his mind.

154

Fuck. What did I say?

"Are you serious?"

Shane shrugged, no longer confident enough to open his mouth.

Chris sighed and looked away for a moment, leaving Shane wishing he could read his mind. "And here I thought you were one of the rare people who actually get what it means to be bisexual." Chris sounded tired and not a little frustrated. "It's not as if I have a switch in my head I can just flip at will, you know. I don't wake up in the morning and decide who I'm going to be attracted to that day while I have my first cup of coffee." Chris gave Shane a hard stare before lowering his gaze to the table top and the empty container he was pushing around.

"That's not what I meant," Shane said. "I just figured that if you refrained from getting into a relationship with a man you'd be bound to eventually find yourself falling for a woman." Of course, if he were totally honest he'd have to confess that he'd never really given the whole concept a lot of thought.

To his credit, Chris appeared to be giving the idea some thought before reacting. When he did his voice was thoughtful and sad.

"You know what? It's possible it could work that way. I have no idea. But I'm not sure it would be a risk worth taking. Why would I give up on a man I'd fallen for in the vague and uncertain hope that I'd walk into a woman I would feel as deeply about? What if it never happened? Would you be prepared to give up on happiness to pursue a what-if scenario?"

Isn't that what I've been doing? Lost for words and not sure how to react for fear of making the situation even worse, Shane turned his attention to the playground, searching for Danny and Maya among the throng of running and playing kids. When he couldn't locate them his heart stopped.

Chapter Nineteen

Chris spun the small plastic container, concentrating hard on its circular path across the table top. Shane's assumptions left him devastated. He'd been so happy when he'd gotten no reaction whatsoever when he'd first mentioned his bisexuality. It wasn't as if he wasn't used to people's misconceptions — he'd been dealing with those for most of his adult life. But to have the illusion that Shane did get it and that it didn't matter to him destroyed in such a brutal fashion shattered something inside him.

"Fuck! Where are they?"

Shane's outburst brought Chris back to the present.

"What?"

"The kids! I don't see them anywhere."

Shane was on his feet and off running before his words fully registered with Chris, leaving him to play catch up. Panic coursed through him as he followed Shane, scanning the playground as he went.

Caroline would kill him if anything had happened to Maya. Fuck that. He wouldn't be able to live with himself if she'd been hurt while he was minding her.

"Danny!" Shane shouted. "Maya! Daa-nny!" The alarm in Shane's voice rose to a higher level every time he roared their names.

Chris felt the eyes of the other adults on him as he weaved his way through the playing kids and he could hear their thoughts. *How careless.* And, *some people shouldn't be allowed to be in charge of children.* Anxiety tightened his chest and his eyes burned. *Where are they?*

"Excuse me, mister."

It took all Chris' patience not to growl at the about eight-year-old boy addressing him. "Yes?"

"Are you looking for a boy and a girl?" the lad asked in a small voice, clearly intimidated by Chris' size and demeanor but still brave enough to speak.

"Yes!" He squeezed his hands into fists and forced himself to be calm for a moment. "Yes, I am. Did you see them?"

The boy nodded. "They're in that house there." He pointed at a playhouse in the corner of the cordoned-off playground.

"Thank you." Chris resisted the urge to hug the boy before rushing off to check inside the small, brightly colored house, vaguely aware of Shane following him.

"Little buggers." As he muttered the words he heard Shane say 'thanks be to God' behind him.

One glance through the open doorway had shown him Danny and Maya fast asleep on the ground. He pulled his phone from his pocket and took a picture. Despite his retreating fear and anger he had to admit they made a cute pair, cuddled up together as they were.

"So much for endless supplies of energy I guess," Shane said, sounding as relieved as Chris felt.

"We'd better get them out," Chris said. "It's not that warm in the shade and I'm sure Caroline won't look much kinder on me for returning her child with a cold than she would if I did manage to lose Maya."

They took their time waking the kids up, smiling when both of them grumbled as soon as they were told they'd be going home.

"Can Maya come home with us, Uncle Shane?" Danny asked. "She wants to see my *Star Wars* Lego."

Shane glanced at Chris, uncertainty clearly written on his face. "Do you have time to come with us?" Shane hesitated before adding, "I wouldn't mind talking a bit more if that's okay with you."

The refusal sat on the tip of Chris' tongue. The hopeful little faces staring up at him combined with the wordless plea in Shane's eyes forced his hand. He'd probably end up regretting it but...

"Sure. Caroline won't come for Maya until seven tonight. We have time."

The journey back to Shane's house was a subdued affair. Either the kids hadn't fully woken up yet or they sensed the atmosphere had changed since they were quiet and obediently refrained from running as the four of them walked in silence.

The reprieve was short-lived. As soon as Shane opened the front door to his house Danny grabbed Maya's hand and pulled her along as he ran for the stairs, the two of them shouting and giggling as they ascended.

Chris followed Shane inside feeling out of place and confused. He pushed the door shut and waited for Shane's next move.

He didn't have to wait long. Shane stepped closer and looked up at him.

"I'm sorry. I'm an ignorant fucker who doesn't know when to keep his mouth shut."

Before Chris could think of a reply Shane pressed his lips against Chris' mouth and kissed him. He felt torn. Kissing Shane, feeling his body pressed up against his was just right, as if he belonged there. And yet those words kept on tumbling through his head – 'If you hook up with a woman you could solve that problem in about nine months.'

When Shane pulled back, Chris couldn't help wondering if that had been the last time he'd feel Shane's lips against his own.

"We need to talk." Shane's gaze bored into Chris' eyes as he spoke.

"I guess we do," Chris agreed, dreading the upcoming conversation as much as he knew they needed to have it.

Shane led the way to the living room and indicated for Chris to sit while he flipped a switch on a white box sitting on a shelf. Children's voices filled the room instantly.

"This way we can keep an eye, or rather an ear, on them

while they're in Danny's room."

Chris nodded and lowered himself to the couch, thinking that it wouldn't be easy to have a conversation with that chattering going on in the background.

As if he could read Chris' mind, Shane lowered the volume on the intercom before turning to him again. "Want a beer?"

Chris hesitated before deciding that one beer wouldn't impair his childminding abilities. The thought almost made him groan. Having managed to lose Maya, even if it had only been for a few minutes, was a clear indication that he had a lot to learn when it came to taking care of kids.

"Sure. I'd like one."

Shane handed Chris a can when he returned from the kitchen before lowering himself to the couch too, keeping enough distance between them that they couldn't accidently touch each other.

"I really fucked up, didn't I?"

Shane looked and sounded about twelve years old and Chris stayed quiet, not sure what to say.

"I didn't mean to imply that you should use a woman just to have a child together. Or even that you should walk away from someone because you can't have a child with them." Shane stared at his hands as he talked. "It's just that for me, as a gay man, the thought of children never crossed my mind. And on the rare occasion I did think about it, it was more in relief that whatever happened I would never accidentally get a partner of mine pregnant." He glanced up at Chris before averting his gaze again.

He allowed the words to sink in. They made a weird kind of sense. Chris wanted to believe Shane hadn't meant to be cruel. But between what he'd said and the way he'd been keeping Chris at arm's length it was hard not give into the suspicion that he'd been imagining a bond growing between them. Maybe it was time to stop pussyfooting around. Chris sighed and reached out to place a hand on Shane's thigh.

"Tell me what you want."

"I don't know." Shane bit his lip while staring at the can in his hand as if it could provide all the answers he needed. "I mean I know what I think I want but I don't know if I should be wanting it or even if I can deal with it in the long term."

Chris squeezed Shane's leg, earning him a grateful smile in return, but stayed quiet, waiting for what Shane might say next.

"I'm not a big believer in lasting relationships. My father disappeared when I was still a child. Danny's father did a runner before the boy was even born. And who needs that shit? Getting all attached to someone only for them to up and go again. It's much easier to push someone away than to wait for them to do the pushing." Shane placed his hand over Chris' and stroked his skin with his thumb. "See, I don't know what it is about you but even on that first night in the pub I couldn't make myself do my usual routine and just disappear as soon as we'd both climaxed."

He at last lifted his gaze to focus on Chris, his eyes blazing with a passion Chris couldn't identify.

"And then when you showed up in VikInk I figured you'd drop me like a hot potato as soon as you'd talked to Troy. But that didn't happen either. And now…"

Shane stopped talking and Chris knew he wouldn't continue without prompting.

"And now…?" Chris asked the question as gently as he could.

Shane sighed. "And now I'm not sure that I want you to disappear anymore. There are so many reasons why this" —he waved his hand between the two of them before returning it to its previous position—"is a bad idea."

"Give me one of them," Chris demanded, unable to keep quiet.

"Danny," Shane answered. "He's just lost his mother. I don't want him getting used to having you in his life if you're just going to disappear again."

Chris ignored the flash of anger he experienced. Shane didn't know him well enough to know whether or not he played for keeps and after the stunt his own mother had pulled, Chris could understand where Shane was coming from.

"You know how long it's been since I was last in a relationship?"

Shane shook his head.

"Almost nine years. Maya's mother was the last." Chris thought for a moment. "I have never been careless about relationships. That's what hook-ups are for." He grinned at Shane who returned the expression.

"I understand why you worry about Danny. And we don't know each other well enough to know if we're going to work together." He hesitated before continuing, trying to figure out how to best put into words what he wanted to say next. "May I suggest something?"

"Sure," Shane said.

"We could take it slowly. We don't have to indulge in displays of affection in front of Danny. I could refrain from spending the night here." He thought it out as he spoke.

"Would *you* be okay with that?" Shane asked before Chris could continue. "It's all well and good me putting restrictions on myself because I'm now responsible for Danny. You're under no such obligation."

Chris smiled. This one was easy. "I am if I want to be with you."

"It doesn't leave a lot of time for us."

Chris wondered if Shane was trying to discourage him or just pointing out the pitfalls before they fell afoul of them.

"So we'll have to try harder to make time, and make sure that whatever time we do get is well spent." Chris wondered whether he was fighting a losing battle.

"Yeah." Shane's face lit up. "That could work. In fact..." A slight blush crept up his neck toward his cheeks. "My mother offered to take Danny off my hands next weekend — something about her not wanting me to stop living just because I'm now his guardian."

Chris grinned. "See! Some things are meant to be. That's my weekend off." He focused his attention on the sounds coming from the intercom, making sure both kids were still upstairs and playing relatively peacefully together, before bending forward and claiming Shane's mouth.

The response was instant. Shane parted his lips and pushed his tongue against Chris' until he gained entry. There was nothing soft or subtle about this coming together. They were greedy and demanding, their tongues battling as if they were in a contest. Low growls escaped both of them. Chris wasn't sure how it had happened but he didn't complain when Shane suddenly sat on his lap, straddling him and pushing as close as he could get. He wrapped his arms around Shane, stroking his back before pushing his hands down and squeezing his arse cheeks.

Sudden silence from the intercom combined with footsteps on the stairs had them scrambling to separate again. When Danny and Maya walked into the room Chris could only be grateful that they were too young to wonder why two grown men would be out of breath while apparently sitting peacefully on the couch.

"We're thirsty," Danny announced.

"I guess I'd better fix that," Shane answered.

Chris checked the time while Shane was busy in the kitchen and was disappointed to discover it was quarter past six. If he wanted to be home and have Maya organized before Caroline came to pick her up at seven, he'd have to leave soon.

Ten minutes later Chris and Maya turned in the street and waved at Shane and Danny who stood in the doorway of their house.

"Did you have a nice day?" Chris asked Maya.

"Yes!" She grinned up at him. "It was fun. Danny's nice. We're going to get married when we grow up."

"Sounds like a plan," Chris said, while wishing that establishing an adult relationship was as simple as it appeared to kids who were still oblivious to the obstacles life could and almost invariably did throw up.

Chapter Twenty

"Are you sure you won't join us for a pint?"

Shane turned to face Barry and considered the question for a moment. The Fridays when he didn't have to rush home to make sure he got to spend some time with Danny before the boy had to go to bed would be few and far between, so maybe he should join his colleagues for a quick drink. On the other hand there was Chris. Which meant it really wasn't a choice at all.

"Sorry. No can do."

"Fair enough. Have a good weekend," Barry said.

"And you." Shane opened the door and walked away from VikInk with a spring in his step he hadn't experienced in months. For a moment he felt guilty about the feeling of freedom he experienced. He loved Danny and most of the time the boy was delightful company, but God, how he craved adult conversation. *And not just conversation either.* The thought put a huge grin on his face.

He strolled the streets, the heavy weekend bag he carried not burdening him, unable to wipe the smile off his face. The sun was shining, he had two days off and after weeks of belly-aching and denying an attraction that refused to die he would at last find out if the bond he felt between himself and Chris extended beyond more or less platonic interactions.

Well, he sorta already knew the answer to that question. The first time he'd met Chris had proven that they were very capable of creating magic together. The smile broadened and much to his surprise passers-by smiled back at him, as if his happiness was contagious.

He turned into Muckross Parade, marveling at how perfectly it all seemed to fit. If he'd believed in signs, he would have taken this as confirmation that some things were just meant to be. Just like Shane, Chris lived within walking distance from city center and both their jobs. More than that, the hike from Ballybough, where Shane lived, to Chris' house took only just under half an hour.

As he rang the doorbell, pleasurable nerves churning in his belly, he decided that while he knew better than to trust providence he was willing to believe that maybe his luck was beginning to turn.

"There you are." Chris opened the door sporting a grin to equal Shane's. "Come in. I only just arrived myself."

Shane crossed the threshold, put his bag down and was ready to proceed down the hall when Chris grabbed his upper arm and turned him around.

"Not so fast. I've been looking forward to this all week."

Before Shane could reply, Chris had claimed his mouth, devouring it with a hunger matching Shane's. He surrendered to the heat, his body relaxing as Chris pushed him until his back connected with the wall.

Had he really thought he'd be able to give up on this for ten years or more? Who had he been trying to fool? He grabbed Chris by the back of his neck and pulled him closer, needing to feel the press of that big, strong body against his, relishing the way Chris' bulk enveloped him as the play of their tongues awakened all of his nerve endings, making his skin feel alive and his cock press against his fly.

Chris pulled back and Shane reluctantly opened his eyes to find himself staring straight into Chris' large pupils.

"Are you hungry?" Chris sounded hoarse.

"Only for you." Shane wanted to cringe at the cheesiness of his answer until he recognized the answering desire in Chris' gaze. He'd given the right reply.

"We'll eat later so." Chris took his hand and pulled him toward the stairs.

Shane felt giddy from a combination of anticipation,

nerves and pure raw heat. He followed Chris up and into the bedroom before his feet stopped moving. *We are really going to do this.* Chris turned to face him as soon as Shane's lack of further progress registered.

"Are you okay?"

Shane nodded.

"We don't have to do this," Chris said without a note of frustration or judgment in his voice.

The words were enough to snap Shane out of his sudden stupor.

"We do." He growled the words and closed the distance between them. He lifted his chin and offered his mouth to Chris again, whose reaction was instant and resolute.

Shane's mind went blank as he lost himself in Chris' mouth, his tongue and the large hands exploring his body, stroking his back, squeezing his arse and pulling him ever closer. His body screamed for more, closer and, above anything else...

"I want to feel your skin." He murmured the words against Chris' lips when they both came up for air.

Chris stepped back without a word and pulled his shirt over his head. When he turned to drop it over a chair Shane inhaled sharply. When he'd spent the night in Chris's bed weeks ago, he had somehow managed to miss what he saw now. He'd been curious about Chris' lack of visible tattoos. His back answered any questions he might have had.

Shane forgot about his own clothes as he stepped closer to Chris and traced a finger over the outlines of the myriad of images on his back. It felt like a summary of someone's — probably Chris' — life story. There on his left shoulder was Australia, while Ireland featured on the right-hand side. In the middle, as if it grew up his spine, was a tree with bare branches on Australia's side and bright green leaves on the other. The *kanji* crowning the tree captured Shane's attention.

"What does it mean?" His voice was barely more than a whisper.

Chris didn't hesitate a moment before answering, obviously certain which tattoo Shane meant.

"Renewal. I had it placed to signify the transition from my old life Down Under to the new one I'm building in Ireland."

Renewal. How fitting. Shane stored the information away for future reference, convinced that the word was as meaningful for him as it clearly was for Chris. He stared at the large tattoo as a whole again. The image provided a thought-provoking contrast. There were so many more images, too many to decipher at first glance, but what struck Shane most were the spots remaining empty.

"You're still creating your story."

For the first time since Shane had touched his back Chris moved, looking over his shoulder.

"I am," he said with a sigh. "I'll keep on telling it for as long as I live."

"Australia hurt you more than you're willing to admit." Shane made a statement rather than asking a question.

Chris shrugged. "That's more a thing of the past. It was true when I created the design."

Shame filled Shane. He'd been so caught up in his own drama that he'd never even considered that Chris might have his own demons. He pressed his lips against the naked branches, wishing he could take the bleakness away with just his lips and tongue.

"Enough." Chris turned around, unbuttoning his trousers while his heated gaze travelled up and down Shane's still fully dressed body. "You're falling behind."

Shane laughed and rushed to catch up with the man who'd be his lover in a few minutes. He forced himself to ignore the fact that Chris was stripping less than a meter away, certain that he'd forget about his own clothes again if he allowed himself to watch. Only when he was fully naked did he focus on Chris again and almost stopped breathing.

Despite his best efforts to not allow Chris to get under his skin, he'd fantasized about what he might look like naked.

Reality was so much better than anything his imagination had been able to come up with.

The wide shoulders didn't come as a surprise and neither did Chris' broad chest, but the thick covering of dark hair did. Shane reached out and stroked through the fur, marveling at how soft it was. Since he was there anyway, he brushed a finger over one of the nipples, relishing the resulting sharp intake of breath.

Chris was big but he didn't appear to have an ounce of unnecessary fat on his body. His waist was slim and the trail of almost black hair running downward from his navel drew Shane's eye to...

He bit back a moan. He'd known Chris was well built in the groin area too, but had somehow managed to forget exactly how well. His cock was large and half erect, practically begging for the attention it needed to get to full mast.

Without thinking about it, Shane dropped to his knees and leaned into Chris' upper thigh, resting his cheek against it, smiling when hairs tickled him. He breathed in the smell of Chris, savoring it as he did the opportunity to be up close and very personal with Chris' private parts. He pressed his slightly parted lips against the root of Chris' dick, caressing it with the tip of his tongue, while vaguely aware of a hand coming to rest on the back of his head.

This was new. He'd never taken his time with another man. His past experiences had been fast and furious, demanding and almost brutal.

He wetted his lips with his tongue and slowly moved his mouth up. He gripped the skin with his lips, licked it and pressed soft kisses against the growing organ. Every time he felt it jerk the movement elicited a similar reaction in his own dick.

"Fuck, man, you're killing me."

Chris sounded hoarse and delightfully needy. Shane wished he had the patience to continue teasing him indefinitely but his own need was growing, becoming ever harder to resist.

When he reached the tip of Chris' cock he lapped at it, treasuring the pearl of pre-cum he captured before sucking the head into his mouth and swirling his tongue around it.

"Yes. God...yes!"

Chris tightened his grip on Shane's hair, urging him on without actually being forceful. Not that he needed the encouragement. He craved this. His whole world revolved around the desire to give Chris pleasure. He wanted to hear him lose control, make helpless noises, beg, demand.

He took him deep and called on all the experience he had. *I'll make this special. You deserve special.*

His own dick throbbed on top of his thighs and he was tempted to take himself in hand before realizing that he wanted these moments to be just about Chris. He could wait.

It wasn't long before Chris met the movements of Shane's mouth with short pushes of his hips. Shane relaxed, allowing Chris to set the rhythm, taking what he was given and using his tongue to its best advantage.

Chris' breathing came in short, sharp bursts and Shane sucked and licked harder, longing for the moment Chris would lose it.

"Not yet." Chris slowly withdrew his cock from Shane's mouth before gripping his upper arm and pulling him up. "Your mouth should come with a health and safety warning."

Shane didn't have a chance to think of a reply before Chris slammed his mouth over Shane's, devouring him while simultaneously pushing him until the backs of his knees hit the bed.

A gentle push against his chest and Shane fell, his heartbeat skipping before he landed on the soft covers on top of the comfortable mattress. He looked up to find Chris staring down at him, his gaze raking over Shane's body, hunger shining from his blown pupils.

He swallowed hard, his mouth suddenly dry. *Nobody*

has ever looked at me like that. But then, he'd never wanted to please someone as desperately as he wanted to satisfy Chris.

Chris lowered himself to the bed, hovering over Shane and resting his weight on his hands on either side of Shane's head.

Shane pushed his body up, aching to get closer to Chris, to feel his skin, to have those hairs tickle him. Frustratingly, as Chris lowered his head to kiss Shane, the rest of his body moved away from rather than closer to Shane's.

The kiss was sensuous instead of demanding and Shane lost himself in it, closing his eyes to truly savor the sensation. The moan escaping him when Chris' lips left his should have been embarrassing but he didn't care. As Chris kissed his way down Shane's body, teasing his nipples, bathing his bellybutton, nerve endings Shane had never known existed burst to life, raising delicious trails of goose pimples.

Chris bypassed his cock to lick his balls before sucking one into his mouth, rolling his tongue around it before switching to the other one. Shane yearned for Chris to take his straining dick into his mouth while dreading it at the same time. He had no idea how long he'd last and he didn't want this to end.

"Turn over."

Shane obeyed wordlessly, certain that right now he'd do anything Chris might ask of him.

He loved the firm grip of Chris' large hands on his arse cheeks. He pressed up into the squeezing fingers. Lips against the top of his crack surprised him. Hands spread him followed by teasing kisses trailing a path down Shane's cleft.

He shook, the sensations almost too much, too intimate to bear.

Tender lips stroking over his hole drove him wild. Shane squirmed under the onslaught of pleasure, the movement creating a delicious friction for his rock-hard dick.

He vaguely registered one of his arse cheeks being released

before he heard a squirting sound. Then a finger pressed into him, slowly. The burn was slight, the sense of rightness overwhelming. He pushed back, silently demanding more and getting it when a second finger joined the first.

"God but you look good." There was enough heat in Chris' voice to start a fire.

Shane's body buzzed, sensations swirling through him, pushing him higher. Chris' fingers drove him out of his mind. He couldn't think anymore. He was reduced to want and need and something close to desperation.

"I want you." The words came unbidden and almost as a surprise.

"Are you sure?" Chris' fingers stilled. "We don't have to do this."

Shane pushed his arse up, chasing the friction he craved.

"I want you." He growled the words, no longer in any doubt about the truth behind them.

When Chris withdrew his fingers Shane bit into the bedcover to stop himself from cursing. *I'm not going to make him do something he's not into.* But, God, he wanted the connection as he'd never wanted anything before. The sound of a drawer opening and closing followed by foil being torn reassured him.

Chris' cockhead pressed against his hole and Shane remembered vividly exactly how well-endowed the man was before his hole was breached and all thought left him as his universe narrowed to that small part of his body.

The burn was sharp but ended almost as soon as he felt it. Chris pulled him up until the back of Shane's head rested against his shoulder before withdrawing his cock and pushing back in.

"So good."

Shane agreed but couldn't get himself to speak.

Suddenly careful wasn't good enough anymore. Shane moved with Chris, demanding harder, faster, more.

"This is going to be quick." Chris sounded as strained as Shane felt.

"Yes." Shane growled. "Do it."

Chris took Shane's dick in his hand and matched its movements to the ever more forceful pushes with his cock.

Shane couldn't remember the last time he'd bottomed and wondered what had been wrong with him. Why had he deprived himself of this pleasure? Then he remembered. He'd always felt that unless he topped he would be relinquishing control and he'd had no intention of doing so with the men he'd routinely picked up. This was different. This was Chris. Suddenly it hit him. What he was building with Chris had the potential to go way beyond a good bond. He wasn't in lust. *God help me, I'm falling in love.*

His orgasm crashed into him and for the first time in his life he actually did see stars.

Chapter Twenty-One

Chris woke slowly, awareness creeping in leisurely as he luxuriated in a feeling of well-being and pure, golden happiness. At first his brain was too foggy to latch on to the reason for his euphoria, until he rolled over and encountered a warm body next to his.

Shane. He opened his eyes and something quivered in his stomach when he saw Shane's head on the pillow next to his. The room was half dark, early morning rays filtered by the heavy curtains covering the windows, created an interesting pattern of light and shadows on the man's features.

Chris resisted the urge to reach out and touch Shane, allowing him to sleep on while indulging in this opportunity to observe him in private.

Something had shifted in his world the night before, something that both scared and delighted him. He no longer had any doubts. He'd known there was something about Shane since the moment he'd first set eyes on him in the pub. He'd trusted his instincts despite Troy and Xander's warnings and in the face of Shane turning subsequently hot and cold on him. He'd had no idea how deep it went nor did he understand how this *something* could have grown into an overwhelming feeling of rightness, of belonging. But now that he'd found it he would hold on tight, treasure it and give it every opportunity to grow further.

Shane stirred and turned onto his side, facing Chris. Temptation grew too strong and he reached out and stroked a finger along Shane's jaw line, tracing the stubble there. The beautiful man next to him frowned in his sleep, his lashes fluttered and he opened his eyes, squinting at Chris. The smile on Shane's face when he realized where he was and what—or maybe who—had woken him up warmed Chris.

"Good morning," he said in a soft voice.

"Morning." Shane sounded cute, his voice husky with sleep.

"Come here." Chris pulled Shane on top of him and tugged him close. God, this felt so right. The night before had been mind-blowing, hotter than he could have imagined and without a doubt the most intense sexual experience he'd ever had, but this? This was perfection.

"How do you feel about morning breath?" Shane murmured the words against Chris' neck, his breath tickling sensitive skin.

"As long as we're both unbrushed, I've no issues with it."

Shane sniggered. "Unbrushed? Is that even a word?" Before Chris could think of an answer Shane lifted his head and pushed his lips against Chris' mouth. He languished in the comfort Shane's soft kisses brought him. He didn't want to push or demand. Tender, slow and easy felt perfect to Chris. The illusion that they had all the time in the world, that life wouldn't start making its demands again all too soon, seduced him.

Shane shifted his weight and their cocks brushed over each other, sending a spike of lust up Chris' spine. He grabbed Shane's arse and kneaded the cheeks. As he'd hoped it resulted in Shane squirming against him.

Shane took the kiss deeper, his tongue demanding as a low growl escaped his mouth.

A shrill ringtone broke the spell.

"What the fuck? Who's calling me at eight on a Saturday morning?" Chris stretched his arm out, grabbing his phone from the bedside table. He checked the screen before answering.

"Troy?"

Shane stiffened on top of him.

"I'm sorry, Chris. I know it's your day off and that you

have plans, it's just..."

Chris was shocked to hear a note of panic in Troy's voice. "What's wrong?"

"It's Xander. The eejit went to change a light bulb and fell off the chair he was standing on. There's something wrong with his hand. I need to get him to a hospital."

"You need me to come in." Chris stared into Shane's eyes, reading the question there all too fluently. So much for having a full day together before real life would kick their butts again.

"If only to contact the people who have appointments today and cancel and reschedule them."

"Nah, it's okay. If I come in I might as well keep as many of them happy as I can. You get Xander to an X-ray machine and I'll take care of the rest."

"Thanks, although you're going to have to make one cancelation. I'll leave the details out. This customer was very specific about needing to talk to someone capable of creating original art for him to cover his scars. You'll have to tell him that while Xander can talk to him at a later date, you're not sure when he'll be able to produce samples."

Chris glanced at Shane, an idea forming in his mind. He'd be taking a risk. He wasn't sure how Troy *or* Shane would react to his suggestion, but it made sense. And if it worked...

"Shane is here with me." Chris left it there, hoping that Troy would pick up on his meaning.

"I figured as much. That's why I said that you don't have to take these bookings. Just reschedule them."

"That's not what I meant. I'll be quick because you're in a hurry." Chris took a deep breath and mentally crossed his fingers. "Shane could talk to that client of yours. He's more than enough of an artist to provide any information the man needs and I know he's familiar with and admires Xander's art, so he could probably be fairly specific about what is and isn't possible."

Shane raised his head from Chris' chest and glared at him

while the phone against his ear remained silent.

"Is Shane willing to do that?" Troy asked after what felt like an eternity.

"Would you do that?" Chris asked Shane. "Xander has injured his hand and needs to go to A&E."

Shane stared at him, his face expressionless. Just when Chris was sure that not only was Shane going to say no, he would probably also storm off, he nodded.

"Sure. I can do that."

"You heard?" Chris spoke into the phone.

"I did."

"Okay. Go and get Xander sorted. I'll talk to you later." Chris pressed the 'end call' button before Troy could react and turned his attention to Shane.

"I'm sorry I dropped you in it like that."

"It's okay," Shane said. "I owe him. Fuck. I owe both of them." He looked away. "I'm not looking forward to seeing him again, but this I can do. And with a bit of luck the waiting time in the hospital will be so long we'll be long gone by the time they get back."

Pride filled Chris. He'd been right all along. No matter what Shane had done in the past, beneath it all he was a more than decent man.

"Thank you, I appreciate it." What he really wanted to tell Shane was how proud he was of him. Both of them knew that chances were Troy and Xander would be back at the parlor long before Pins & Needles closed at the end of the day and he'd still said yes. That took balls and Shane had proven there was nothing wrong with his. Chris suppressed the snigger bubbling up. After all, last night he'd had first hand — and first tongue — experience of the rightness of Shane's balls.

* * * *

They entered Pins & Needles shortly after nine. Chris watched Shane as he allowed him to cross the threshold

176

first. He walked a few steps into the parlor and came to a halt, studying his surroundings.

"He's been upgrading the place." It was a statement, not a question. "The artwork on the walls is stunning. All Xander by the looks of it." Admiration was clear in Shane's voice.

"You've been here before?" Chris asked.

"Yes, once." Shane suddenly appeared very interested in the gothic figurines Troy kept on his counter. "It wasn't one of my better moments." He glanced at Chris before diverting his attention again. "Then again, none of my interactions with Troy over the past two years have been what you might call positive experiences." He held up his hand as if he wanted to stop Chris from interrupting him. "And yes, all the negativity has been on me." He turned to Chris, confusion shining from his eyes. "I can't even explain to myself why I thought I could behave like that. How am I ever going to make it up to Troy? Why should he accept an apology? Back then I didn't think about any of it twice. Now I can't stand the person I used to be."

Chris knew he should be checking the diary for appointments and preparing for the first customer, who would more than likely turn up before too long, but this was more important.

"Come here." He spread his arms in an invitation and Shane stepped into them.

"Don't worry about it now. We'll just deal with the work ahead. But you know Troy well enough to realize that he's a reasonable man. I'm not going to say you didn't hurt him. I'm not even going to pretend it wasn't a bastardly thing to do."

Shane flinched against him and Chris stroked his back to reassure him.

"But you're not that man anymore. The fact that you're here proves that. The way you're dealing with Danny is further evidence, if any were needed." Chris lifted Shane's chin and forced him to look at him. "It's good that you recognize your mistakes, but it doesn't make sense to martyr yourself over them. You can't change what has happened. All you can do is make sure you don't repeat the past." He pressed his mouth against Shane's, brushing their lips together before reluctantly stepping back.

"And now I'd better check what I'm up against today. Why don't you go through there" — he pointed at the internal door — "and make us some coffee. If I don't get some soon I may just end up hurting someone."

Shane studied him intensely for a few moments before nodding, turning and following his suggestion.

＊ ＊ ＊ ＊

Four hours later, Chris locked the door after the last morning client had left. The first part of their day had been busier than the diary had predicted. Apart from the appointments already in the book, two spontaneous walk-ins had arrived too. Initially, Chris had been inclined to book them in for another day or refer them to another parlor. When Shane had offered to set the small tattoos those customers had requested Chris had agreed. Only now did it occur to him that Troy might be less than happy that he'd allowed Shane to use his equipment. But it had been done and the machine had been cleaned and returned to where it belonged. If there were repercussions, he'd deal with them if and when they happened.

"If you put the kettle on, I'll go and get us something to eat."

When Chris returned with the sandwiches and crisps he heard Shane talking in the back rooms.

"I'm not sure, Ma. I'm helping Chris out in the tattoo parlor where he works and he needs me to be here this afternoon. Are you sure it can't wait?"

Chris frowned when he heard the words but made sure to relax his expression again before entering the kitchen. Shane turned to him, a worried expression on his face.

"What's up?" Chris mouthed the words silently.

"Hang on for a moment, Ma." Shane covered the bottom of his phone with his hand.

"Something has come up, although she won't tell me what." Shane scowled. "But the long and short of it is that she needs me to take Danny for a few hours this afternoon."

Fuck. This was inconvenient to say the least. It was too late to cancel the appointment with Xander's client now, but if he arrived only to find his journey had been in vain he might be upset enough never to return. Losing Troy what promised to be a very big commission would be bad, but it was more than that. Chris had hoped this might be an opportunity to start a reconciliation between Troy, Xander and Shane. If Shane had to renege now his boss and his partner would only take it as further proof that Shane couldn't be trusted.

"Can she drop Danny off here?" Maybe, Chris hoped, it didn't have to be complicated.

"Here?" Shane stared at him as if Chris had lost his mind.

"Sure," Chris said with more confidence than he felt. "It's only for a few hours. The one client you need to deal with is coming at a time without any other bookings. So one of us can keep Danny occupied while the other is busy." He thought about having the curious boy around and grinned. "I bet he'd love to see what you actually do for a living and how it works. The only problem I foresee is explaining to him why he'll have to wait at least another eleven years before he can get a tattoo himself."

"Are you sure?" Shane looked torn between relief and doubt.

"One hundred percent."

Shane moved the phone back to his ear and explained the plan to his mother.

"Okay, see you then," he said after he had given her directions to Pins & Needles.

Chris handed Shane his lunch before making them both a cup of coffee. The afternoon promised to be interesting, to put it mildly. But Danny was a good kid and between the two of them they shouldn't have any problem keeping him busy. If the worst came to the worst there was a television in what used to be Troy's living room. Besides, it wasn't something Chris was prepared to confess to yet, but he liked the boy and enjoyed spending time with Danny. With a bit of luck this too could be turned from an inconvenience into an opportunity.

Chapter Twenty-Two

"I can't see any reasons why you wouldn't be able to get exactly the art you're looking for."

The customer studied the drawings Shane had created and grinned. "Thank you. This is more than I dared hope might be possible."

Pride filled Shane. He'd agreed to take on this project because he felt it was the least he could do after everything he'd put Troy and Xander through and because it made him feel good about himself to help Chris. Okay, and also because he really hadn't wanted to cut his time with Chris short. Goodness only knew when they'd be able to arrange a weekend together again.

I do want more one-on-one time with Chris. The realization came as a shock and made him wonder whether there actually was such a thing as karma. He'd never looked for prolonged interactions with a partner when he'd had all the time and freedom in the world to have them. It was somewhat ironic that now that Danny took up most if not all of his free hours he suddenly found himself longing for the opportunity to develop a relationship with Chris.

He pushed the thoughts away. He still had a customer to deal with.

"Does Troy have your contact details?" he asked the man.

"Sure he does, why?"

"You expected to design your art with Xander. I am familiar with his methods and images and what we created today is very much in line with those, but I wouldn't be surprised if the artist himself would like to make a few suggestions for improvements."

The man thought for a moment before nodding. "That's fair enough. They can email me any further ideas, but right now I can't imagine how even Xman might improve on this." He tapped the paper.

"Wow. That's stunning."

Chris' voice coming from behind him took Shane by surprise while his words filled him with warmth. As far as he knew Chris had been keeping Danny occupied in the back room.

"My thoughts exactly," the customer said before glancing at his watch. "I need to go." He stood up but didn't take his eyes off the drawings on the counter. "I wish I could take those with me."

"Why don't you take a few pictures with your phone before you go?" Shane suggested. "Xander and Troy will need the originals, but there's no reason for you not to have the images too."

The man pulled out his phone and took numerous shots before shaking Shane's hand. "Thanks. It's been a pleasure working with you."

"You're very welcome, and likewise." Shane was half surprised he meant what he said. He'd expected to feel frustrated about creating a design which he wouldn't be able to finish completely, but instead he was proud of what he'd been able to do rather than resentful over what he'd miss out on.

"You did well," Chris said as soon as the customer left Pins & Needles, the pride in Chris' voice filling Shane with warmth.

"You think so?" He cringed when he realized how needy his question sounded. Chris' approval mattered far more to him than Shane was willing to admit even to himself.

"Where's Danny?" Shane asked, grateful he had a legitimate reason to steer the conversation away from the work he'd just done.

"Come." Chris smiled. "I'll show you."

Shane followed Chris and couldn't stop himself from

smiling too when he found Danny fast asleep on the couch in the back room and the television on with the sound lowered.

"I'm sorry about the lousy timing."

Shane's mother had arrived with Danny about five minutes after his client had walked in and he'd been forced to leave it to Chris to talk to her and supervise Danny.

"There's nothing to be sorry about. Danny knows me. He and I had a great hour together. Wait till you see the drawings he made for me before he crashed."

"He wanted to draw?" Shane was surprised.

"Probably because he saw you working," Chris said with a smile in his voice. "He couldn't stop telling me how great your pictures are and that he wants to be just as good as you are."

Shane's heart filled with a sense of pride he'd never experienced before. *Danny looks up to me.* "Show me."

"They're in the kitchen." Chris led the way. "There." He pointed at the table where three large sheets of paper covered the whole surface. "I'm making a cuppa while we have a moment. Want one?"

"Hmmmmm?" Shane only half listened, already studying the drawings. "Sure."

The first two pictures didn't take him by surprise. Danny had drawn a playground in one and a cat in another. Shane smiled. Danny always drew cats. It was his less than subtle hint that he really wanted a pet. The third drawing, however, pulled him up short. *Shit.*

"I guess it's true," he muttered, not sure whether to be happy or scared about what he saw.

"What's that?" Chris turned away from the counter where the kettle was just beginning to make bubbling sounds.

"Did you look at these?" Shane asked.

"Of course I did. I sat next to him as he drew them."

"Did you make suggestions about what he should draw?" Shane wasn't sure whether he hoped Chris was behind this particular image or if he wanted it to be all Danny's initiative.

"Nope. Those are all Danny's — ideas and execution."

"So how did he come up with this?" Shane pointed at the image of two clearly male stick figures holding hands. One of the men was significantly larger than the other and sported what Shane assumed was supposed to be a beard.

"I have no idea and I didn't ask him. Does it worry you?"

Am I worried? Shane had no idea how he felt about what Danny had drawn. He knew his sister had told Danny about Uncle Shane liking men more than women because she'd wanted the boy to grow up used to the idea before he was old enough to realize that most of the world did not pair up like that. He wasn't worried about Danny drawing him holding hands with a man so much as concerned that he'd clearly done what he could to make the second figure resemble Chris.

"I'm not sure," he admitted honestly. "I'm not sure how he picked up on it...on us."

"Can't help you there," Chris said. "I know next to nothing about children or how they experience the world. But I do remember Caroline telling me how Maya is forever surprising her with the things she picks up on even when she's trying to make sure the child is unaware of a situation." He glanced over his shoulder at Shane. "You're still concerned that Danny will get attached to me?"

He already knows me so well. The thought warmed Shane but not enough to stop him from asking the question. "Should I be?"

Chris stared at him for a moment, an unreadable expression on his face before he turned back to the kitchen counter, opened a cabinet and took two cups down.

"I'm not sure what you expect from me."

Shane stared at Chris' back, wishing he would turn around so he could study his features while completely understanding why he didn't.

"If you are waiting to tell me that we are going to spend the rest of our lives together, you'd better not hold your breath."

Shane deflated. He'd been right to be cautious if Chris was already thinking about how whatever it was they had together would end again.

Chris put coffee granules in the cups, adding sugar to one of the mugs while he continued talking, addressing his words to the wall and sink in front of him. "But that is exactly what I want. I can see a future for you, me *and* Danny. When he drew that picture, I don't know, I felt as if he was telling me something, as if he was welcoming me into his world."

Shane cursed the fact he couldn't see Chris' face. He sounded choked up.

"But if you're not there, I get that," Chris continued. "We haven't known each other that long. You've been through some major upheavals in your life. I understand why you are careful about doing anything that might create more turmoil for Danny or for you."

The kettle boiled and turned itself off and Chris poured water into the waiting cups. The aroma of coffee filled the kitchen.

"What I'm trying to say is…" At last Chris turned around, his gaze fixed on the two cups in his hands as he took the few steps separating him from the kitchen table before putting them down. "I'd never knowingly hurt you or the boy. I'm…" Chris swallowed hard. "I'm falling for you— have been since the first time we met. I don't think I've ever felt like this about anyone before. But none of that comes with guarantees."

"I know." Shane pushed his fear aside, determined to be honest no matter how scary that was. "You make me want things I've never been interested in before. I'm feeling things I thought only existed in movies and books. I thought I knew what I should be doing, but I guess I don't know anymore." He studied the picture again. It was so tempting to take it as a message, to interpret it as Danny giving him permission. He snorted.

"What?" Chris asked.

Shane shook his head. "I must be in trouble if I'm looking at a five year old for approval." He wrapped his hands around a mug and lifted it to his mouth, allowing his thoughts to flow freely while he drank. If Danny had already made the connection was there any point in trying to create an artificial and unwanted distance between himself and Chris? Would he only confuse the boy more if he pretended Chris was just a friend without a significant role in their lives?

He pushed the questions aside for the moment. If he wanted answers he'd have to talk to Danny and that was a conversation he wasn't quite sure how to have. Besides, he hoped that Chris might be able to throw light on another mystery.

"Did my mother tell you why she needed us to mind Danny this afternoon when she dropped him off?" Shane was still frustrated he'd been busy and unable to talk to his mother before she left again.

"Not really," Chris replied. "She told me something had come up and she needed to meet someone to clarify a situation. I didn't feel I could press her for more information."

"No, you couldn't." Shane felt very uncomfortable not knowing what was going on. "It's just not like her to go back on her word. I'm worried something might be wrong."

Chris reached out and took Shane's mug from his hands before pulling him into his arms and Shane relaxed into the comfort he found there.

"You can ask her when she comes back. She said she shouldn't be later than five o'clock. That's less than an hour away." Chris' voice and words were as comforting as his embrace was.

"When's the next appointment?" Shane asked.

"In about half an hour." Chris pressed his mouth against Shane's for a languid and undemanding kiss. "We don't have to figure it all out this afternoon, you know. I truly believe we'll be okay as long as we're honest—with each other and with Danny. I know he's only five, but clearly we need to give him credit for being more perceptive than we ever suspected."

When the doorbell rang out, announcing the arrival of someone, Chris relaxed his hold. Shane cursed to himself. For a few all-too-short minutes he'd felt completely content and safe.

"Chris? Where are you?"

Shit. So much for getting out of here before Troy and Xander return. A cold sweat broke out in Shane's armpits.

"You stay here for a moment." Chris brushed his lips across Shane's before releasing him and turning toward the shop.

"On my way, boss."

As Chris headed for the parlor Shane wondered whether the day could possibly get any more stressful. Between his growing feelings for Chris, his mother dropping Danny off here and the boy's perceptiveness, he had enough on his plate to worry about. He didn't want his first conversation with Troy to take place with Danny around. Chris would have been bad enough, but he was an adult and fully aware of the situation. If Troy decided now was the right time to have it out with Shane once and for all, Danny would witness the whole debacle. Shane couldn't come up with a single scenario in which that would end on a positive note.

Feeling restless and nervous, he drained the coffee cups in the sink then washed and dried them. He examined the drawings one last time before rolling them up and walking to the room where Danny was still fast asleep. He'd need to wake him up soon or the boy wouldn't sleep at all tonight.

Voices reached him from the parlor, tempting him to approach the connecting door and listen in on the conversation despite his common sense telling him he might not want to hear what was being said. He'd long since lost the fear that Troy's opinion of him might influence Chris. If it hadn't happened weeks ago it was unlikely to do so now. And Shane wouldn't blame Troy if he held on tight to the anger he felt toward him. That didn't mean he wanted to hear Troy's justifiable resentment toward him first hand though.

Another glance at his nephew made up his mind for him. He was ready to face Troy's wrath if that was what awaited him, but he wouldn't do it with Danny present. He slowly made his way to the door, relieved to have come to a conclusion. He'd listen to determine what the atmosphere was like. If it felt hostile he'd take the boy and go.

Chapter Twenty-Three

Xander and Troy stood at the shop's counter when Chris entered the parlor, studying the designs Shane had created and left there. Xander's right hand and lower arm were in a plaster cast.

"Well, he always was good." Troy sounded begrudging.

"That's better than just good," Xander said, his voice a combination of admiration and surprise.

"Hey, you're back." Uncomfortable to be listening in on a conversation that might not be meant for his ears, Chris made his presence known. "You managed to do some real damage then," he added when Troy and Xander turned to face him.

Xander scowled. "It's a pain in the fucking arse, not to mention my arm. And don't get me started about hospitals. I thought I'd never make it out of there again."

"Stop sulking." Troy smiled at his boyfriend. "It is what it is and we've survived the emergency department." He turned to Chris. "How did you get on today?"

"Fine," Chris said. "No major issues at all. Two unexpected customers who Shane was willing and able to accommodate, and that client" — he nodded at the drawings — "was delighted when he left." He closed the distance between himself and the two men and studied the drawings with them.

"I'm not surprised he was happy, these are good." Xander traced one image with his left index finger. "If I didn't know any better…" He didn't finish his sentence.

"What?" Chris asked, ready to come to Shane's defense if necessary.

"This is very close to what I would have drawn. Not just the idea, but also the style. It's uncanny in fact."

Chris opened his mouth to respond but had his words cut off by a voice coming from behind him.

"That was the whole idea."

Shane's voice was soft, as if he was afraid that just speaking up might cause offense.

Xander and Troy exchanged a look Chris couldn't decipher before turning to face Shane.

"What do you mean?" Xander asked.

Chris' heart went out to Shane, who had to be very uncomfortable under the scrutiny. *And probably feeling isolated right now.* Chris spun around and took a few steps until he stood beside Shane. As much as he didn't want Troy and Xander to think he'd turned against them, he couldn't bear the thought that Shane might feel abandoned.

"I figured if the man asked for a consultation with you it was probably because he likes your art, so that's what I gave him." Shane lowered his gaze before continuing. "Or at least, I tried to stay as close to what I thought you would have done as I could. I'm no artist, not of your caliber anyway."

Chris wanted to shout at Shane and tell him to stop putting himself down but realized he needed to stay silent. No matter how much he wanted to stand up for Shane, this was something that could only be resolved — or not — between the three other men.

"I like it." Chris picked up on a trace of reluctance in Xander's admission. "Can we talk about these for a moment?"

"Of course," Shane replied.

Chris' heart went out to him. Shane had made it perfectly clear he hoped to do Troy and Xander this favor without actually having to meet them and they'd almost gotten away with it. On the other hand, Chris wanted the matter resolved if that was at all possible. He didn't want to feel bad about this job when he was with Shane, or forced to not mention his boyfriend while he was at work.

"Why don't you two go to the back and talk there?" Troy said to Xander and Shane. "You can fill me in on the rest of the day," he added, looking at Chris. "Just give me a moment. I've been bursting for a piss for ages."

Shane, Xander and Troy trailed each other through the internal door and Chris suddenly found himself alone with too many thoughts running through his head. He wanted to stay close to Shane, just in case he needed support while talking the designs through with Xander. If he had his way he'd sit the three of them down and keep them there until they'd talked all their differences out. He had no illusions about Troy and Xander ever becoming close friends of Shane's but surely all of them were grown up enough to be civil.

He wasn't sure why he felt so queasy about it now. He'd known from the start that being close to Shane might and probably would create tension and he'd decided he could deal with it, that getting to know Shane better was well worth any resulting discomfort. Except that now that he found himself facing what that meant in practical terms, he wasn't sure what he would do if the confrontation he'd almost forced Shane, Troy and Xander into blew up in his face.

"You want to explain why there's a kid asleep on my couch?"

Troy's voice shocked Chris out of his increasingly dark thoughts and he forced a smile onto his face as he turned to face his boss, who stood in the doorway, leaning against the doorframe.

"That's Danny. He's Shane's."

"Shane's?" Troy looked dumbfounded, his eyes wide and his mouth open in an almost perfect circle. "He has a child?"

"Yes," Chris said, "or rather no. Danny's his sister's son."

"The poor little bugger." Troy turned his head and studied the boy for a moment. "I didn't know she had a child."

"Shane's the boy's guardian now."

The shock on Troy's face was understandable. "That's a bit of a mindfuck for someone who's incapable of making or sticking to long-term commitments."

Chris understood Troy's cynicism. If anybody had the right reasons to mistrust Shane it was him, but the comment still got Chris' hackles up. After all, it might not constitute a relationship, but Chris was fairly sure Shane and he had been exclusive for over a month now. And Shane hadn't run. He'd wanted to, Chris had no doubt about that, but the important part was that he'd stuck around. What was more, after the previous night and that morning, Chris had started to hope Shane might be willing to at least talk about a relationship. He bit back on his temper and dug deep for a reasonable tone and choice of words.

"For someone who used to be unable to commit you mean. All of us have to grow up at some point." He shrugged. "So, it took Shane a while longer than most."

Troy said nothing, pushed away from the doorframe and walked toward the counter before facing Chris again. "I'm sorry. You're right. But it's going to take me some time to get my head around the new and apparently much improved version of Shane I'm afraid."

"Listen. I get that he's never going to be one of your favorite people. But I care about him." For a moment Chris wondered whether or not he'd end up regretting saying the words burning on his tongue. Then he realized that no matter what the cost, he'd feel worse if he stayed silent. Taking a deep breath to calm himself and not sound aggressive, he continued.

"He didn't have to accompany me today. I didn't make him come or pressure him into working with that customer. He's here because, in his own words, he owes you." Chris forced himself to stay calm. "I'm sorry, Troy. I know this isn't my fight, but I'm so tired of having to defend both myself and him every time he's mentioned in a conversation I'm having with you."

Troy stared at him without saying a word before nodding.

"Fair enough. I told you I wouldn't hold your relationship with Shane against you and I meant it." He picked up the diary and flicked through it, studiously avoiding looking at Chris. "I...eh." He swallowed. "I called that customer before we left the hospital. I wanted a firsthand report on how it had gone."

"That's not unreasonable," Chris said although part of him was disappointed that Troy had apparently decided his judgment couldn't be trusted.

"I know you wouldn't have lied to me if it hadn't worked out for whatever reason but..."

Chris resisted the temptation to ask 'but what' and waited.

Troy faced Chris and smiled. "You are right of course. The man couldn't praise Shane enough. He's so delighted with both how Shane worked with him and with the results that I feared he wouldn't be happy working with Xander next time he comes up."

"I thought his next appointment is only ten days away," Chris said, confused. "Will Xander be able to draw again by then?"

"No. That's going to be a matter of weeks, not days." Troy stared at the door to the back of the building. "I'd better talk to Shane."

Worry churned in Chris' stomach. This was exactly what he'd had in mind when he asked Shane to come with him today, but now that the moment had arrived he could see so many potential pitfalls that he suddenly doubted the wisdom of his idea. Not that his second thoughts made a blind bit of difference. It was out of his hands now.

Chris glanced at the couch as he followed Troy to the kitchen, instantly noticing that Danny was no longer sleeping there. Delighted laughter sounding from the kitchen solved the mystery of where the lad had disappeared to.

Troy stopped walking before entering the kitchen and Chris was grateful his height advantage allowed him to view the sight in front of them over Troy's shoulder. Xander and Shane sat side by side at the table, with Danny kneeling on a chair on the other side.

"What if we'd...?" Xander pointed at something Chris couldn't see.

"Like this?" Shane asked.

Chris sighed a breath of relief. Whatever would happen between Troy and Shane, it was clear that Xander and Shane at least had found common ground in their art.

Troy moved again until he stood behind Xander. "How are you getting on?"

He put his hand on Xander's shoulder and bent forward to inspect what they were doing.

Chris didn't even think about it before he copied Troy's movements except that Shane was his point of arrival. He wasn't trying to turn this into a stand-off but he was determined to make sure Shane felt neither outnumbered nor isolated right now.

"Very well," Xander said with a surprised note in his voice. "I have one or two suggestions for minor adjustments but other than that, I can't say I would have designed the images differently."

Chris softly squeezed Shane's shoulder, immediately noticing the tension in his body.

"I've asked Shane to come back for the client's next appointment." Xander stared up at Troy and Chris turned his head to study him as well, wondering what Troy's reaction might be.

"Actually." Shane sounded hesitant. "Before I agree to that, could I have a word with you, Troy?"

Chris didn't miss the frown flashing across Troy's face before he responded.

"Sure. Do we need to take it somewhere private or can you say your piece here?"

Chris wouldn't have thought it possible, but Shane's muscles tightened further under his hand. Suddenly the tension in the room was so palpable even Danny picked up on it. He slid off his chair and walked around the table before squirming his way onto Shane's lap.

Shane wrapped an arm around his nephew, pulling him close, then lifted his chin and faced Troy. "I apologize." He glanced at Xander. "To both of you, of course, but," he addressed Troy again, "mostly to you."

Chris held his breath as he waited for Troy to respond but he just stood there, the neutral expression on his face not giving any clues as to what he might be thinking.

"That's it. I've got nothing else. I was a selfish bastard and a prick. You deserved better and I'm glad you got there despite my thoughtless efforts to undermine you."

"But..." Troy said, clearly unconvinced.

"No 'buts'," Shane countered. "There are no excuses and I'm not going to try and make some up."

Chris wanted to wrap his arms around Shane and tell him how proud he was of him but limited himself to flexing his fingers on Shane's shoulders again while he waited for what came next.

"I'm glad you made it despite my betrayal." Shane's gaze never left Troy's face and Chris wondered how hard that had to be considering that Troy's expression gave nothing away.

"I think you did better on your own than we could ever have done together. I know it doesn't change anything, but maybe what I did worked out for the best for you in the end. I hope so."

Once again silence settled on the room. Even Danny, who had always talked a mile a minute whenever Chris had been around him, kept his mouth shut. Chris studied Troy's features, searching for something that might indicate what he thought of Shane's apology.

Eventually it was Troy who broke the deadlock and turned away from Shane, a half-smile the only indication that a crisis might have been averted.

"Okay." Troy sighed. "I hear you. And I believe that you are sorry. I'm grateful for what you did today. I would have hated to lose this customer and now I won't. But I'm afraid that's all I have right now."

"I'm not expecting anything from you," Shane said. "I'm glad I could do this. I hope you won't give Chris a hard time for…" He gazed up at Chris.

"I wouldn't," Troy immediately said. "I told Chris from the start I had no intention of telling him who he could or couldn't spend his time with."

"Does that mean you will come back?" Xander asked. "I want to combine all of these" — he pointed at the collection of images on the table — "into one large design, but…" He held up his hand and scowled at it. "Besides, I had my opportunity to get rid of my anger months ago. I guess I owe you an apology too."

Shane rubbed his nose and grimaced. "Nah, I deserved that, even if it did fu…hurt like hell." He took a deep breath and continued. "Provided we can fit it in around my job and Danny, I'd be happy to come back and finish this job with you. And not just because I owe you two."

Chris felt Shane relax under his hand when the bell in the shop rang out and a ringtone sounded at the same time.

"I'll take this last client," Troy said before leaving the kitchen while Shane extracted his phone from his pocket.

"It's me ma," he said before answering, suddenly frowning again.

Chapter Twenty-Four

"Why did you have to leave Danny with me today, Ma?"

Shane really wasn't in the mood for yet another heavy conversation but it appeared to be the day for all of them. When his mother had called him earlier it had been to tell him she wouldn't be able to collect Danny until seven, so he and Chris had brought Danny back to Chris' house until she was ready to pick him up.

"No reason, son."

Her tone of voice almost convinced Shane but he knew his mother better than that. She'd never go back on a promise unless she thought she had a very good reason.

"You're talking to me, Ma, not Danny. Out with it."

It was rare to see his mother uncomfortable and not quite sure of herself. Despite the cooling evening Shane was glad they were having this conversation in Chris' garden, out of earshot of both Danny and Chris.

"Danny asked me where you were and when I told him, he was so disappointed he wouldn't get to see Chris too that I figured…"

A lifetime of not cursing in front of his mother kicked in and Shane took a deep breath before responding.

"Didn't you think I might have my reasons for not allowing Danny to get too used to Chris?"

"The thought did cross my mind." She smiled at him affectionately. "And I'm fairly sure I even know what your reasoning is. I just happen to think you're wrong."

"What?"

"How are you ever going to figure out whether or not you and Chris might have a future together if you don't include

Danny in the process? He's an integral part of your life now. You two have become a package deal, so it's only fair to give Chris the opportunity to find out what a relationship with you *and* Danny would mean for him." She glanced through the window into kitchen and Shane followed her gaze.

"Look at them," she said as they both observed Danny and Chris doing the washing up. With Danny in charge of the washing it meant soap bubbles and water were fast soaking both the floor and the boy.

"Whether you like it or not, those two have started to bond. When Danny's football training kicks off, Chris will be in charge. Hiding what's happening between you and Chris is only going to confuse the lad."

"Jaysus, Ma. I've only known Chris for just over a month. This, whatever this is, is so new. What if Danny gets used to him and it doesn't work out?"

"And when was the last time you stuck with someone for a whole month?" His mother glared at him. "Or the first time for that matter."

That shut him up.

"I get that it's new and scary." His mother's tone and face had softened again. "And God knows I'm only too aware of the emotional turmoil you've been through. But look at him." She once again directed his attention to the kitchen, just in time to see Danny pull a glass of water from the sink and in the process drown Chris, who didn't bat an eyelid but scooped up some suds and flicked his hand so they fell on Danny's hair. The boy's loud laughter rang out into the garden.

"I want you and Danny to be happy and I think Chris is good for both of you. Don't worry about the boy. He's far more resilient than either of us gives him credit for. Don't stop living because you're now raising a son, Shane."

For the second time in less than five minutes, Shane was lost for words. *A son.* He hadn't allowed himself to think of Danny as anything other than his nephew, but his mother was right of course. For all intents and purposes Danny was his son. He waited for the panic to kick in and was surprised when it didn't. Maybe his subconscious had copped on to the idea long before he had allowed the thought to enter his mind. The same subconscious that had stopped him from pushing Chris away when he'd been so sure it was the only logical thing to do.

"Okay, Ma, message received loud and clear." A thought struck him. "You weren't going to leave him with us tonight, were you?" Shane realized he didn't even know whether Chris had cleared out his spare bedroom since the last time Shane had been in his house. If not, there'd be nowhere for Danny to sleep.

"No, I had never any intention of doing that. And if the two of you want to spend another weekend together without a lively five year old underfoot, all you have to do is tell me. I think I made my point."

Shane embraced his mother and hugged her hard. "Thank you, Ma. I think."

She kissed his cheek when Shane released her again. "That's okay, son. It's my job to make you see sense when you're being silly. Look and learn. It won't be long before you'll have to do the same for that munchkin."

* * * *

"Are you okay?" Chris handed Shane a can of beer before sitting next to him on the couch and pulling him close.

"Sure," Shane said before realizing he might as well be honest. "Somewhat overwhelmed, but yeah, I'm not bad."

His mother and Danny had left a few minutes earlier to loud protests from the boy. In the end Chris and Shane had had to promise they'd take him to the zoo next weekend just to get him to go with his granny without making a scene.

"I'm not surprised." Chris took a sip of beer. "Even I am still trying to make sense of everything we've been through today." He drank some more. "Did you ever find out why your mother needed us to mind Danny?"

Shane laughed softly. "Oh yeah, did I ever."

"Nothing to worry about then?" Chris sounded relieved.

"That depends on your point of view I guess, but there's nothing wrong with her."

"Stop talking in riddles and tell me what's going on," Chris demanded.

"Apparently Danny thought it wasn't fair I got to spend the weekend with you and he didn't, and me ma agreed."

"He did?" A huge smile spread across Chris' face.

It really makes him happy. Some of the anxiety Shane had felt when he'd learned how attached Danny had already become to Chris dissolved in the face of Chris' obvious delight.

"But it worries you," Chris said, not even bothering to put it as a question.

"That he likes you?" Shane asked. "No, I'm delighted the two of you get on. Kids often have the best instincts when it comes to judging people and I can't imagine being in a relationship with someone Danny didn't like or who didn't get on with him."

It was only when Chris pulled him in closer that Shane realized he'd used the word 'relationship'. He opened his mouth to take the word back again, to moderate what he had said before deciding against it.

"I want to be in a relationship with you *and* Danny," Chris said. "But I understand why the idea scares you."

"I'm not afraid of being in a relationship with you." Shane wondered how to explain his thoughts without upsetting Chris. "I'm no longer that man who prefers to be on his own."

Chris chuckled. "I know, you don't have to convince me of that." He loosened his grip on Shane's upper arm. "Look at me." His tone had turned serious again.

Shane turned his head and stared into Chris' beautiful dark brown eyes. "I know and understand that you worry about Danny getting attached to someone who might not stay for the long haul, especially so soon after having lost his mother."

Chris' voice was calm and without hurt or negativity, and for the first time Shane truly believed Chris really understood his concerns.

"I've said this before. I can't guarantee that we'll last forever."

Shane opened his mouth to interrupt Chris but he talked on as if he hadn't noticed.

"But then neither can you. That's not how relationships work." Chris leaned into Shane and kissed him before continuing. "What I can assure you of is that I'll never intentionally hurt the boy. No matter what happens between us, I do not want him to suffer, not now and not in the future."

Something lifted inside Shane, as if a weight that had been burdening his heart had been removed. As much as he wanted guarantees, he knew Chris was right – some things happened without conscious efforts on the part of those involved.

"Tell me something," Chris said. "I know it probably sounds stupid, but I've had this feeling of rightness ever since that night we met in the pub, as if the two of us meeting was inevitable. Don't you feel the same?"

Shane allowed the words to play through his mind before realizing that if he were honest and ignored all the fears and doubts he'd been dealing with ever since then, Chris had just hit the nail on its head. The reason the idea of Chris had scared him for so long was because he'd known from the start that it wouldn't be a casual fling.

He took Chris' can from his hand and put it, together with his own, on the table before straddling Chris. He wanted to be able to see all his reactions while they had the rest of this conversation.

"Are you sure?" He had to know for certain. "It doesn't scare you to take on me *and* the boy? Kids cramp your lifestyle, there's no avoiding that. You might end up resenting that." What he didn't say was that deep down

Shane was worried he'd end up fed up because his social life had been taken away from him.

Chris put his hands on Shane's hips and pulled him closer. "Yes, I am sure. I'm thirty-five, Shane. Sure, I enjoy a good night out, but my days of living the highlife are over. I've been there, I've done that and now I'm ready for what comes next." He pressed his lips against Shane's and kissed him almost harshly. Shane's body reacted instantly, as if a switch had been pushed in his brain. He was very aware of his cock filling and the nerve endings in his skin coming alive. It wouldn't be long before Chris turned him into a mindless mess of want. He had one more thing he needed to say before that happened. With great difficulty and reluctance he pulled back from the kiss.

"You realize that even if we do make it work it won't be all plain sailing?"

"Relationships never are," Chris said.

"And we'll be two men raising a young boy. Marriage equality and adoption rights for same sex couples may be a fact now, but that doesn't mean everybody is going to approve of us."

Chris shrugged and for a moment his apparent lack of concern worried Shane. If he couldn't see the potential problems or didn't care about them...

"There will always be people who don't approve of others for whatever reasons. In a way we're at an advantage because we already know what the issues will be long before we have to deal with them. We can prepare for what we may face, we can give Danny the confidence he'll need to deal with whatever he may encounter."

Shane had never thought about it like that but it made sense. The problems they might well run into could be predicted and therefore dealt with before they happened.

"Let's not over-think this," Chris continued. "I agree that we have to keep Danny in mind as we move forward, but we shouldn't rush things. We'll take our time. Give all three of us the opportunity to get used to the new situation. Because you are right. We don't know each other that long or that well." He pulled Shane closer still and pushed his hands underneath Shane's shirt, stroking over naked skin and awakening heat and need with every touch. "And there are so many parts of you I want to get better acquainted with."

Shane relaxed, the last tension leaving his body. He didn't think he'd ever stop worrying about Danny and whether or not he was doing right by the boy, but he figured that was a burden every parent had to bear. And he couldn't deny that he took comfort in the idea that he wouldn't be trying to figure it all out on his own, that he'd be able to share some of the burden and responsibility. He knew, without a doubt, that he did trust Chris to not hurt him or Danny intentionally. The miracle was that Chris appeared willing to believe the same about him despite Shane's track record. He laughed.

"What's so funny?" Chris muttered the words against Shane's neck which he'd been kissing and nibbling.

"I just realized that if one of us has good reasons to worry about the trustworthiness of the other, it is you, not me."

"None of that, please." Chris' voice was low, sounding almost like a growl. "If I didn't trust you I wouldn't be here. I'm nobody's masochist."

No, you're not. But you are my miracle. Despite knowing the words to be true, Shane couldn't say them out loud, not yet.

"And now." Chris interrupted Shane's thoughts before he could get too lost in them. "Now I want you naked and in my bed." He grinned. "I want to explore some of those parts of you I don't know well enough yet."

Chapter Twenty-Five

Chris allowed his gaze to roam over the naked man lying on his bed, drinking in his features while being seduced by just the sight of Shane. One day he'd take his time to study all the individual tattoos on his stunning body, but it wouldn't be tonight. He was curious whether Shane's art also told a story, but the need to know faded into insignificance compared to the urge to be close, for skin on skin contact, to taste him and to give and receive pleasure.

"Are you just going to stand there and look at me?" The expression on his face made it clear Shane was going for a cocky attitude but his hoarse voice betrayed his desire.

"I like looking at you," Chris said. "You're gorgeous like this, spread out in front of me, on display and waiting for me to give you what you need."

"You think you know what that is?" Shane asked with an uncertain note to his voice.

Maybe better than you do. Chris didn't say the words. There was no need for Shane to know that he could sometimes see the lost little boy in Shane's eyes. Right from the start Chris had suspected Shane's sometimes brutish exterior hid an uncertain man who hadn't yet figured out exactly what his place in the world was. He cherished the opportunity he'd apparently been given to prove to Shane that here with Chris — in this bed *and* in his life — was exactly where he belonged.

His gaze lingered on Shane's cock, which was almost fully erect and continued to fill under his stare. What a wonder to have that happening without touching. Then again, his own dick wasn't far behind.

Without thinking about it he wrapped his hand around his cock and gave it a few leisurely strokes. Shane's sharp intake of breath did far more for his excitement than his own touch did.

Chris lowered himself to the bed, draping his larger body over Shane's slight but solid frame. He made sure to catch the weight of his upper body with his arms while allowing their groins to connect.

Shane's reaction was instant. He pushed his hips up, grinding his erection against Chris'.

God, he wanted the man, all of him.

Chris smashed his lips against Shane's, pushing his tongue into Shane's mouth before he ended up saying things he shouldn't mention yet. Their tongues stroked, caressed and attacked. Giving and demanding, wordlessly asking questions and supplying answers. Nothing had ever felt as right as this moment did. Chris had been so reluctant to give Shane any guarantees but in that moment he didn't have a single doubt, couldn't imagine ever not being with this man.

Shane squirmed underneath him, causing flash after flash of pure pleasure to shoot through Chris, driving his desire higher.

Reluctantly he pulled back from the kiss. He could have kept it up forever, couldn't imagine ever getting enough of the taste of Shane, but he wanted more. There were too many parts of Shane's body he hadn't explored yet. He looked down and his gaze locked on Shane's nipple piercings. Those, for example, were very tempting.

He scooted down the bed and latched his mouth onto one of the tiny buds, teasing it with his tongue, scraping his teeth over it before biting down and pulling.

"Fuck me." Shane's breathless curse was like oil to an already raging fire.

"Not tonight," Chris muttered while he switched nipples.

No, not tonight. Chris wanted to feel Shane inside him this time. It occurred to him it was a conversation they'd never had, but given what he knew about Shane's past he couldn't imagine the man not topping.

Shane's nipple hardened under the subtle torture Chris exposed it to. The sounds coming from Shane's mouth providing any encouragement Chris might have needed.

He licked, sucked and nibbled his way down Shane's body, longing to get a taste of what he'd denied himself the first time. When his lips closed around Shane's cockhead the man underneath him trembled.

"Jaysus, Chris, you're killing me."

I haven't even started. He couldn't make himself extract his mouth to actually say the words.

In one fluent move, he swallowed Shane, keeping his nose nestled in Shane's pubes until his lungs screamed at him. He slowly pulled back before sliding his lips down again.

It didn't take long. Shane squirmed underneath him, meeting the movements of Chris' mouth with jerks of his hips while the sounds escaping him betrayed both his need and his excitement.

God, this felt good. Shane's responsiveness fueled Chris' desire and spurred him on. He'd drag this out, bring Shane to the edge and back down again. He wanted Shane to be borderline out of control by the time he got him to fuck Chris hard.

"Not yet." Shane growled the words as he pushed Chris' head away from his cock. "I want this to last," he said moments later when he'd managed to regain some of his breath.

Chris moved up Shane's body again and pressed his mouth against Shane's, allowing his lover to share the taste of his pre-cum, still fresh on Chris' tongue.

"I want you to fuck me," Chris said when they pulled apart for a moment.

Shane stared into his eyes as if he couldn't believe what he'd just heard.

"You do?"

"More than anything."

A slow smile spread across Shane's face. "Get off me."

When Shane pushed against Chris' shoulders he allowed himself to be rolled over onto his back. His head had barely hit the pillow when Shane spread Chris' legs wide and knelt between them.

"Lube. Condom." Shane held out his hand as he made the demand while he used his other hand to stroke Chris' cock with long, languid strokes.

Chris reached to the side, blindly scrabbling for the drawer in his bedside table and thanking his lucky stars when he his fingers encountered the items. He threw them onto the bed in the general direction of Shane before relaxing into the pillow again and losing himself in the sensation of Shane's mouth on his throbbing cock.

Shane took his time, his mouth and tongue teasing Chris rather than pushing him toward completion. When he felt a finger trace a path from his balls to his hole, Chris held his breath. Soft tapping loosened his tight opening some and he yearned for more, pushing back against the finger.

"I like you when you're needy." Shane sounded both delighted and breathless.

"You bastard," Chris murmured affectionately before growling when the tip of Shane's finger breached him.

He surrendered to the sensations, losing himself in the sensual delights provided by the combination of Shane's mouth and finger. He was torn between the urge to close his eyes and just feel and the desire to see Shane and watch him as he reduced Chris to a puddle of need.

The tension in his body rose despite Shane still taking it easy. His balls tightened and he fought the threatening eruption, not wanting this to end yet. It was too good. It had to last.

When Shane released his cock and sat back, resting his arse on his calves, Chris felt torn between relief and disappointment. He watched as Shane pushed the condom down his cock, anticipating the hard length entering his body, wanting it with a ferocity he hadn't experienced before.

Shane stared straight into Chris' eyes as he stroked a lubed hand up and down his own cock. His pupils were blown, his lips parted and his breathing came in short, sharp bursts. Chris had no doubt he looked and sounded exactly the same to Shane.

"Lift your legs."

Chris acted immediately.

Shane's cock pressing against his hole felt right and when he pushed through the muscles and entered him Chris thought he'd encountered perfection.

"All of you," he demanded.

Shane obliged, pushing forward in one slow but smooth movement until Chris could feel his thighs against his arse.

"God but you're tight." A moan escaped Shane. "So good."

Chris was beyond coherent words. He heard the sounds escaping his mouth as Shane moved inside him but he had no idea what they meant.

He'd always suspected he and Shane would be good together. The previous night had been more than he'd dared hope from what for all intents and purposes had been their first unrushed union. This? This confirmed what he'd imagined from the moment he'd first set eyes on Shane — they were something special together.

Then his thoughts stopped too as he was reduced to nothing but nerve endings and feelings.

"Almost there," Shane warned.

Chris grabbed his own cock and stroked in time with Shane's movements. *There.* "Fuck. Again!"

Shane's movements became harsher, more forceful and drove Chris higher until…

"Yes. God. Yes!" Cum covered Chris' hand and belly as Shane shuddered, stopped moving and pulsed deep inside him.

"Fuck me." Shane sounded surprised before he allowed himself to collapse on top of Chris, completely ignoring the sticky mess between them.

Chris didn't care. He wrapped his arms around Shane and pulled him close, wishing he could just keep him there. If he'd had any doubts about the rightness of the two of them they'd scattered in the face of the magic they'd created together.

They lay in silence, catching their breath while occasionally caressing each other. Only when Chris feared he might doze off did he speak.

"Maybe we should clean up," he suggested.

"Are you always going to be sensible?" Shane grumbled.

Chris laughed softly and pressed a kiss against Shane's cheek. "That's unlikely."

"Thank God for small mercies." Shane groaned as he pushed himself away from Chris' body, winking at him as he moved.

"Okay, come on then." Shane stood next to the bed and held out his hand, ready to pull Chris up.

* * * *

Half an hour later they were back in bed. Cleaning up had taken somewhat longer than absolutely necessary but then, that was always a risk when sharing a shower.

Chris couldn't stop smiling. He was happy, his body satisfied and in his arms he held the man he didn't want to let go again.

"Yes," Shane said in response to no question Chris had asked.

"Okay?"

"Yes, I do want to do this. Be with you, I mean. It still scares me but..."

"But what?" Chris asked, cupping Shane's chin and turning his head until they looked at each other.

"I can't convince myself it isn't the right thing to do anymore." Shane sounded surprised.

Gratitude filled Chris and he kissed Shane.

"We're going to be fine. The three of us. We'll take our time. No hurry. No pressure."

"You're really okay with that?"

"Yes," Chris said, the words coming straight from his heart. "I'm more than okay with that. We are new. You've only been Danny's guardian for a few weeks. I've never been responsible for a child. We'll take our time. Get used to each other and figure out what works best." He grinned as an idea occurred to him. "Because we know nothing and all of this is new, we can make it up to be exactly what we want and need."

Shane smiled back at him with trust shining from his eyes. "I think it's going to be fun figuring out what it is that we desire." He lay down and rested his cheek against Chris' shoulder. "I'm looking forward to finding out."

Chris couldn't agree more.

Scenes from Adelaide Road

Excerpt

Chapter One

I took one step forward before retreating again. The wall against my back grounded me, taking some of my panic away. I stared across the street at the door, the bouncers and the slow trickle of people entering the club. I had waited for this moment, dreamed about it for months but now it had arrived I couldn't find the courage to take the last fifteen steps separating me from the threshold.

I forced myself to breathe slowly while I counted up to ten and down to zero again. My body was on high alert, thoughts rushed through my mind and worry cramped my stomach. This was ridiculous. I only wanted to enter a club, discover what it was like on the inside in order to satisfy my curiosity. Here in Dublin, I had no reason to be afraid — there was no one to tell me what I could and couldn't do, and, most importantly, nobody to frown upon me and who

I was.

I was free at last, but I might as well still be shackled to my father and his rules for all the good it did me. I could hear the contemptuous words my dad used to spew at me whenever I'd attempted to create a social life for myself as if he stood next to me. *'Don't make a fool of yourself. Surely by now you've figured out people don't want to be around you. Nobody likes a loser.'* I had hoped the distance between us would diminish his power over my thoughts. I'd been wrong.

Across the road, two more men entered the club. They exchanged a few words with the bouncers and a burst of laughter reached my ears. I studied them. They looked just like me—nothing made them stand out as special or remarkable. Tight jeans, even tighter T-shirts, and loafers. Nothing about their appearance distinguished them from the people who walked past the club on their way to different venues. Nothing, apart from the fact that some of them had been holding hands and others had their arms wrapped around each other, or hands stuffed into each other's back pockets. Nothing, except that couples entering this club were either all male or all female.

That stood out like a red flag in a black-and-white movie. I couldn't imagine ever seeing that back home. The sight filled me with a longing so deep it hurt. I closed my eyes for a moment and allowed the soft June breeze to wash over me. I wanted to believe I could be one of those men one day. Nineteen years of being told I was nothing—not good enough, a disappointment as well as a disgrace—had me convinced my dream would always be that, a futile fantasy.

Time passed and I just stood there. I had to make up my mind—either bite the bullet, cross the road and enter the club or go back home. There would be no shame in going back to my house. I'd only arrived in Dublin two days ago. I didn't have to hurry or force myself. This city was home now. I could visit this club and others like it whenever I wanted, or rather, whenever I found the courage. I half turned to start the short walk home before stopping myself. *No.* If I chickened out now I might never be brave enough to take the first step. Before I could change my mind again I stepped away from the wall, crossed the street and walked up to the door.

"Sorry, mate, we'll need to see your ID."

The bouncer sounded kind enough, but his words still left me fuming inside as I pulled my wallet out of my pocket and handed my age card over. Looking like a sixteen year old when my nineteenth birthday was months behind me sucked.

"Thanks. That's grand. Enjoy your night." The bouncers stepped aside and allowed me to enter the place I'd been longing and dreading to visit in equal measure.

What had I done? Why had I not gone home? Every instinct screamed at me to turn around and walk out again. I glimpsed bright lights, dark corners and a bar along the left hand wall before I lowered my gaze to the floor. I'd seen enough to know the place was relatively empty. A few bodies moved on the dance floor in the middle of the club and some people sat at the tables surrounding it. The music was loud and the beat traveled through my body, making my eardrums vibrate. I didn't look up while I made my way to the far end of the bar where I picked the empty stool next to the wall.

The marble-like surface of the bar wasn't interesting enough for all the attention I paid it, but I couldn't bring myself to look up, never mind study my surroundings. I waited for someone to come and tell me I wasn't welcome. It had happened whenever I'd found the courage to go out in the past and I couldn't believe the same wouldn't happen here. The setting had changed, but I was still the same as I'd always been.

"What can I get ya?" The bartender appeared out of nowhere, or maybe he'd been there all along.

"Bacardi and Coke, please." I whispered the words and wasn't surprised when I had to repeat them so he could hear me over the noise. I took advantage of the bartender having forced me to look up and studied my surroundings while I waited for my drink. The place was dimly lit and divided into various areas. On the far side, couches and coffee tables created comfortable looking seating areas. Near the door, where people were now entering in a steady flow, and at the opposite end of the large space, I saw high tables without seats. The dance floor in the middle of the room sparkled under the spotlights and steadily filled up with swaying bodies.

The bartender had moved back to the center of the bar to fix my drink and talked to a man while he did so, nodding his head when the man stopped talking. Despite the fear churning through my stomach, curiosity took over. Something about the customer with dark hair caught my attention. He was little more than a silhouette but I couldn't pull my gaze away from him until he turned his head and looked straight at me. *Shit.* Muttering the soft curse, I diverted my attention back to the marble top of the bar and traced a dark line with my finger while trying to get my breathing under control. So much for staying inconspicuous while checking out the club. I fought the urge to look back up and establish whether or not the man was still looking at me. *Don't attract attention to yourself.* The voice screamed in my head and I acknowledged its wisdom.

When my drink appeared in front of me on the bar, I paid for it without looking up or acknowledging the barman. I nearly spilled the rum and Coke as I picked it up. The combination of bubbles and alcohol hit the back of my throat as I drained half the cocktail in one gulp. Tears sprang to my eyes and I swallowed hard to keep from coughing. I couldn't do this. Admitting defeat was easier than forcing myself to be braver than I'd ever be. I'd finish my drink and go home. Being alone wasn't easy but I preferred it over the fear and tension keeping me on a knife's edge right now. Maybe once I'd lived in Dublin a while longer, after I'd gotten a better feel for the place, this would be easier. After all there was no hurry. I'd no intention of ever going back home. I had a new place to live and the rest of my life to explore it.

More books from Pride Publishing

Book one in the Dublin Virtues series

Patience is a virtue. But what if you wait too long?

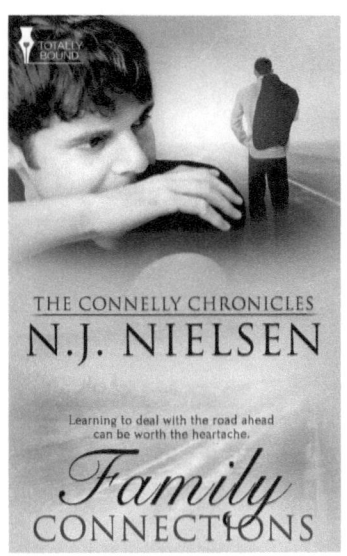

THE CONNELLY CHRONICLES
N.J. NIELSEN

Learning to deal with the road ahead
can be worth the heartache.

Family
CONNECTIONS

Book one in the Connelly Chronicles series

*Ray and Viv realise love isn't always what they expect it
to be, but learning to deal with the road ahead can be worth
the heartache.*

Book one in the Treacherous Chemistry series

Like a depressed moth drawn to a wild flame, Chris hoped
that flame would brighten his life, not burn him alive.

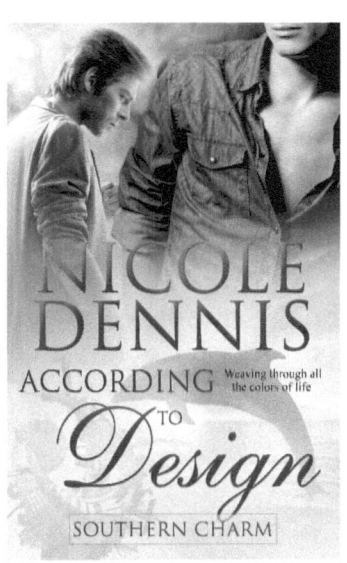

Book six in the Southern Charm series

Amid turmoil and triumph, two men weave through all the colors of life to find one another.

About the Author

Helena Stone

Helena Stone can't remember a life before words and reading. After growing up in a household where no holiday or festivity was complete without at least one new book, it's hardly surprising she now owns more books than shelf space while her Kindle is about to explode.

The urge to write came as a surprise. The realisation that people might enjoy her words was a shock to say the least. Now that the writing bug has well and truly taken hold, Helena can no longer imagine not sharing the characters in her head and heart with the rest of the world.

Having left the hustle and bustle of Amsterdam for the peace and quiet of the Irish Country side she divides her time between reading, writing, long and often wet walks with the dog, her part-time job in a library, a grown-up daughter and her ever loving and patient husband.

Helena Stone loves to hear from readers. You can find contact information, website details and an author profile page at https://www.pride-publishing.com/

www.ingramcontent.com/pod-product-compliance
Lightning Source LLC
Chambersburg PA
CBHW030143200626
46812CB00015B/971

* 9 7 8 1 7 8 6 8 6 1 7 8 8 *